*The U...*

V...

# Save My Sisters

A NOVEL

# L.J. Later

Cover design by j. Caleb

The entire series of *The Untethering* is based on historical events, fictionalized for story-format presentation. Most names, places, characters, and incidents are the author's imagination.

First edition

Manufactured in the United States of America

ISBN-13: 978-1534977105
ISBN-10: 1534977104

*For Stalin's fifty million story-less victims*

# CHAPTER 1:
## *March 20, 1916*

Toppur breaks off a chair leg, places it on the fire and stoops to watch the sparks. He blows softly, the icy vapor from his lips disappearing in the flames. "The elders say this winter is longer than others. There should have been signs of spring by now."

"Go home, Toppur," snaps Rabbi Wecht, throwing off the blanket around his shoulders. "I could be frozen by now if you would stop interfering."

Topper picks up the blanket and rewraps the rabbi. "I will not let you freeze."

"Are you burning your last chair?"

"Better to burn furniture than steal wood from the forest," says Toppur, rubbing his hands together.

"Steal from the forest!" yells the rabbi. "No more wood for the villagers of Kovno! Let the Jews freeze!" He coughs.

Toppur touches the rabbi's forehead. "Do you know what today is?"

"The fifteenth of Adar II, 5676."

"Shame, Rabbi. The Russians forbid our Jewish calendar. Tell me what today is."

"March 20, 1916. Are you satisfied? Now, go home!"

"Today is Purim," says Toppur. "Remember last year's Purim? My mother was alive and your wife was alive and we danced in the square. Purim has always been special."

"And now it's another day of painful, lonely starvation. And that's all."

"No, Rabbi. Purim is a day of miracles. Today the sun will break through the gloom and the villagers will come outside to greet one another and we will all live to harvest."

"I forbid such lies! Now go! Let me mourn for my wife."

"But you taught us to celebrate, Rabbi."

"I was wrong! Almost half the village was killed when we joined together for Hanukkah, including your mother and my Greta. The raiders always watch us. We must stay inside."

"And die quietly? Alone?" Topper shakes his head. "I can't stay inside any longer."

The rabbi spits on the floor. "You are not concerned for the villagers, Toppur. You just want to see the Meinrel girl. You are sixteen and Chana is only fourteen. Slow your passions, boy."

"Chana is beautiful, Rabbi. I know her heritage isn't pure but, before my mother died, she gave permission for the betrothal. I hope you will consent."

"Chana's mother is a gentile, Toppur. You know better."

"I know what the villagers say about the Meinrel family," says Toppur. "Even after fifteen years their tongues still wag about Chana's father going to the city to sell a cow and returning with a gentile wife. Fedora Meinrel might be a gentile, but she's also a doctor. Everyone, even Greta, has benefitted from her skills."

"Enough! There will be no betrothal, and there will be no miracle today. The sun will never shine on Kovno again."

Bright rays burst through the Rabbi's windows, bathing every corner of his house with light. The men squint and Toppur helps the rabbi to the small front window.

The village square lies empty. Looking northeastward, a community well and windmill mark the center of town, just south of a dammed headwater. Continuing down the hillside in a northerly direction, there are sixty-seven rectangular cottages. Last year, before the raids, there were eighty-two. In the rabbi's front yard lay the charred remains of the synagogue.

The sound of a child's squeal breaks the silence. Toppur and Rabbi Wecht bump heads as they peer and leer through the glass, craning and straining toward the noise.

"Over there," says the rabbi. "A little child is running as if he just escaped prison."

A red-haired toddler pumps his short legs across the thawing ground, oblivious of mud flying pell-mell under his bare feet, his arms stretched wide to catch the sun's rays.

Toppur laughs. "It's Otto—Chana's little brother. Look! There's Chana, chasing after him. Just look at her, Rabbi!"

"Exquisite," whispers the rabbi.

Chana leaps deer-like between weedy clumps to avoid the mud and patches of ice. Her dark braided loops slap against her cheeks but she focuses on her target, grabbing hold of Otto's trouser straps.

"Otto, look at you! It's as if you've had no bath," Chana scolds, grabbing one of his ears and guiding him homeward. She doesn't see the faces of her neighbors.

"Did you hear her, Rabbi? They bathed."

"Of course they would bathe, Toppur. It's Purim, after all."

"I must bathe," says Toppur. "Let me help you back to bed."

"The stool is good enough. Go dance."


Across the village square at the last cottage, the Meinrel family's covered back porch bustles with Purim preparations.

Grandmother, Galayna Meinrel, braiding her damp, gray hair, oversees the family's endeavors.

She watches Chana drag Otto onto the porch, pinning the child under her left foot while she ladles fresh water into a metal bowl. Chana sets the bowl of water on the floor and vigorously scrubs her howling little brother.

Galayna assesses Chana, far too beautiful to be ignored. Chana's black hair contrasts with her white skin under those flaming cheeks; strips of burlap cover her feet. Last night Galayna washed the dresses of both her granddaughters—so full of patches it's hard to see the faded brown fabric. Did the dress shrink? How can Chana grow with so little food?

Galayna's sharp senses miss nothing as she pins her braids into tight rounds on either side of her head and pins them. She stands taller than most men, including her husband, Chingas. Deep creases run across her forehead and on both sides of her mouth. Now, as she smiles at her only grandson, the lines and ridges flatten, and she looks younger.

"Chana, love. Leave him some hide," she says, stooping to help.

Otto wails louder, feigning pain, and casts a forlorn look at his father, Ivan. Ivan chuckles and reaches for his mud-splattered son.

"Don't you dare," warns Galayna, and Ivan recoils.

Galayna allows herself to feel pride in her only child, Ivan, even though he married a gentile. It wasn't his fault—Fedora's beauty would beguile any man. The children have their mother's beauty. The Torah says her three grandchildren really aren't hers, which causes Galayna deep pain. Her handsome son, with his large, muscular frame and ink-black hair, made his choice—better than could be found among the village girls, he told her. Fedora, orphaned young, treats Galayna with loving respect. Ivan could have done worse.

Otto looks up at his father, turns down the corners of his mouth and squints tearless eyes. Ivan raises his eyebrows at his son and Otto raises his tiny brows in return. Ivan laughs, and quickly coughs to disguise the forbidden outburst.

Galayna's husband, Chingas, sets a small bundle behind the lye bin. He looks rumpled in spite of Galayna's fussing, and he refuses to allow her to trim his scraggly beard. He smooths his thinning hair only after bathing, which was yesterday. Grandfather Chingas places his dilapidated top hat on his head, ogling his guilty grandson.

"Aha!" Chingas booms. Otto stops squirming and looks at his grandfather. "Grandson, I will never know how you escaped the grasping arms of four women but I pray your maneuvering tactics will serve you long and well."

Otto grins.

"Do not encourage the boy," scolds Galayna.

Fedora and Amalie, Galayna's second grandchild, remove two flats of bread from the fire.

Amalie turned thirteen last month. She styles her hair in braided loops like Chana's. People say they can only distinguish Chana from Amalie if the girls are close together. Chana stands a year taller than Amalie.

"Here, Amalie, hold this bread," says Fedora, pulling a scarf from her pocket and tying it on her head.

Fedora's petite frame, flawless creamy skin and delicate features are in sharp contrast to the Meinrel's broad-shouldered, strong build and dark coloring. She keeps her long auburn hair pinned, forming ringlets on top of her head. Her large blue eyes are generously fringed with dark lashes. Her peasant dress hangs loosely over her small body.

"Is he clean enough?" Fedora asks, poking her loose red curls into her head scarf to hide her glory, as the Jewish law requires.

"Aye, he will do," answers Chingas roughing up the boy's hair. "You go along and greet the neighbors with the women, Grandson. Your father and I have business at the rabbi's house."

"Together?" Fedora asks. "You must not go together. You could be reported. Ivan, please!"

"We'll be careful," Ivan says. "But you and mother and the children need to be quick about your gift-giving. Watchers may know it's Purim. Don't go into anyone's home. Our enemies would certainly call it gathering."

"Gathering!" Galayna snorts, slapping the resistant mud from Otto's trousers with increasing vigor. "For thirty years we cannot visit a neighbor, or speak our language or hear the sacred readings from the Torah. Our children grow up in ignorance."

"Aye, old woman of mine," Chingas soothes, steering her away from his grandson. "But thanks to your grumblings and prayers they know they are missing something. When the time is right they will seek for truth. This evening you may tell us the story of Queen Esther. I, for one, cannot wait to hiss and boo when you describe the wicked Haman. Your stories are much better than the Torah."

"Do not woo me with blasphemy, old man," Galayna says.

Fedora picks up a round bread from Amalie's arms and hands it to her father-in-law. "We made this for the rabbi. Would you tell him we pray for him?"

Chingas holds the bread close to his nose and sniffs broadly. "Perhaps he will have mercy on our words and share it with us," he says.

"Doubtful," says Ivan. "We shall be fortunate if he does not have us skewered."

Fedora puts her hands on her hips. "The rabbi is still in mourning for his wife. His heart is tender. Surely he deserves sympathetic council from the elders."

Ivan meets her gaze. "You are the one with the gift of healing, Fedora. Does not lancing a boil provide relief? As much as we hate to hurt him, we feel the rabbi's spirit needs lancing."

"So, you are taking him sharp words to lance the boil in his heart?" Fedora asks raising her brows. Ivan doesn't answer. "Then be precise, and use plenty of loving balm afterwards."

"Well said, my daughter." Galayna places her hand on her heart and Chingas nods.

"I shall do my best," says Ivan.

Galayna pokes Chingas. "If you hurry home there will be bread to share, as well as some whiskey."

"Is there no end to your enticements?" Chingas says, grabbing his wife and kissing her lips. Galayna swats him, and the children giggle.

"There is a tribute of the Okhrana nearby," Ivan warns. "They may know it's Purim and will look for any excuse to boot our village again. You may greet, but don't linger."

Galayna and Fedora exchange anxious looks.

"Aha!" thunders Chingas, and everyone jumps. Chingas dance-steps to a corner of the porch. "I have made something for my granddaughters," he says. He reaches behind the lye bin and pulls out two crowns of braided reeds. "Crowns for the beautiful queens."

Chana and Amalie rush toward their grandfather, allowing him to crown their heads. They stand back and bow royally. "More beautiful than Queen Esther," he murmurs.

"Where will you girls be?" questions Fedora.

"Toppur will want to walk the path by the river," says Chana, smiling.

"Your betrothal isn't official yet," says Ivan. "Amalie, you go with Toppur and Chana, and all of you stay within the compound. Tell Toppur he is answerable for your safety."

"Yes, Father," Chana says.

"Otto, you can play outside but you must stay around the windmill," says Ivan.

"I will," says Otto. "What's behind your back?"

"It's a surprise," says Ivan, bending on one knee to get eye-level with his son. "A sword to slay the foe, like the Jews in Shushan after Mordacai posted the king's proclamation." He offers a small, dull-bladed carving to Otto, whose eyes grow wide at the gift. The little boy holds the hilt of the sword, grins, and kisses his father.

"And, of course, a royal cape such as King Ahasuerus gave to Mordacai," says Galayna wrapping a patched piece of cloth around Otto's shoulders. The lad looks down at himself, laughs, and kisses his grandmother. He twirls around with his sword outstretched.

"For Moshe Montifiore give a cheer! For Moshe Montifiore give a cheer!" he sings.

"No, Otto. That's a Hanukkah song," corrects Amalie. "You need to learn a Purim song," and she sings, "Beautiful Queen Esther, whose cousin had great zeal, She went unto the king to invite him to a meal. Mordecai, the just, helped her hatch a plan, and saved the chosen people from the wicked Haman. Haman, Haman, hanging on a tree. Mordecai, Mordecai, set the people free, Purim day, on Purim day." Otto tries to join her singing but only catches partial words during the chorus.

The adults hush the children before leaving the porch and walking to the village center. In heart-felt rhythm, doors swing open and villagers greet one another with kisses and exchange meager gifts of food, overlooking the thinness of soups or hardness of breads. Mothers try in vain to hush the enthusiastic singing and dancing children.

Chingas sprints to the far end of town, Ivan at his heels. He passes the charred remains of the synagogue, approaches the back entrance to the rabbi's house and spots Elder Cohen hiding in the shadows, bent and mousy.

"Fedora's right," mumbles Ivan. "Elder Cohen's decision isn't well-timed."

"Nevertheless, he has the calling of president, and we will force ourselves to accept his counsel," says Chingas.

Elder Cohen jumps in front of Chingas and opens the rabbi's door, rapping on it as he calls, "Rabbi, may we enter?"

"What is the meaning of this!" thunders the rabbi. "I did not call for the elders." Rabbi Wecht, usually crisp and impressive, sits on a stool, disheveled and barefoot. He appears much older than his 38 years. If not for his stooped shoulders he might be tall.

"Please, Rabbi Wecht, may we enter?" begs Elder Cohen.

"Wash first. Use the basin. You'll find warm water on the stove, thanks to Toppur for his meddling."

The three men wash and move short-legged stools close to the Rabbi. Chingas and Ivan allow Elder Cohen to sit first.

"And I suppose this is urgent, Elder Cohen — urgent enough to disrupt the prayers of my mourning?"

"Aye, Rabbi. It is most urgent."

"Well? Speak, man."

"We believe you should have a wife," blurts Elder Cohen.

Chingas and Ivan gasp. Chingas watches the rabbi's eyes grow large and horrible; his face and lips drain their color as he sucks for air. The sound of Chingas's pounding heart fills his ears.

"Elder Cohen," the rabbi whispers. "My Greta died just three months ago—burned alive. She was looking for children in the synagogue when the Okhrana burned it. I couldn't save her. I tried, but I couldn't. I see it over and over and over every time I close my eyes. Three months! It feels like yesterday!" Sweat rolls down Elder Cohen's forehead and nose.

Against Chhingas' attempt to shush him, Elder Cohen pants out well-rehearsed phrases, his voice getting shriller with each phrase. "Aye, sir, and she was dearly loved, but the Talmud directs a man to have a wife, particularly a rabbi. You recall the young Rabbi Rosenblatt. When he first came to Kovno you sent him away and told him not to return until he had a wife. You said an unmarried rabbi cannot counsel our women, and you know how much the women rely on a rabbi's counsel. They need their rabbi."

The rabbi squints at Elder Cohen. "There is something with the women that the minyan cannot address while I mourn? What matter is it?"

"It is not one matter. It is all matters." Elder Cohen's voice thins and his hands shake.

Chingas studies the tormented face of Rabbi Wecht. "My friend," he whispers, placing a hand on the rabbi's shoulder. "There is wisdom in Elder Cohen's counsel."

"Chingas, not you! You cannot be in agreement with this," the rabbi pleads.

Chingas nods. "It's hard counsel, to be sure. I was shocked when I first heard the proposal but now I feel differently. Yes, I agree with it."

"How can that be? Greta was all I ever wanted; or needed. Another woman trying to take her place? It would be utterly false and hopeless. It wouldn't be fair to her or to me."

"Maybe there's is a way. Will you allow me to tell you how it might work?" asks Chingas.

Rabbi Wecht stares at Chingas. He puts his elbows on his knees and rests his chin to his knuckles. He exhales, opens his palms and covers his eyes. "It hurts so much. Every day. Every minute. I think, 'if only she hadn't run into the synagogue.' Then I think 'if only I had gone with her.'" A loud sob escapes. "Why did they burn the synagogue?"

"They thought our sons were in it," says Elder Cohen. "They intend to wipe out the next generation of Jews."

The rabbi wipes his face with the blanket. "This burden is too much. I can't bear it. I know I'm not a good rabbi." He rises, walks to the fire, back to his stool, and wipes his eyes. "Go ahead, Chingas, tell me."

Chingas nods slowly. "My friend, when you laid down on your empty bed last night, and awoke in it this morning, what did you feel?"

Another loud sob escapes the rabbi. "Black emptiness. Retching agony," he cries.

"Do you recall your ruling when Elder Minsk wanted to marry again? I believe you said that the Talmud teaches that God also arranges second marriages, and a man's second wife is chosen according to merits."

"That is right, of course, but I am a broken man. I can offer no merits."

"I do not believe you should stop loving Greta, or even that you can stop loving her. Think of how you feel now, and how your soul has suffered these past months." Chingas waits. "Now, imagine that you have a warm woman here, cheering your home, listening to your wishes, placing her arms around you, and comforting you. Consider that she loves Greta too and she also cries for her. You could comfort her and she could comfort you. Would this be good?"

The rabbi tips his head and shrugs.

"My friend," Chingas says, "If the matchmaker could find such a wise woman, who is noted for patience and piety, such a woman could help heal your heart. She would give you the comfort you crave. You are a good husband and she would be the rabbi's wife, deserving of instant respect. You have merits to offer."

Chingas watches the rabbi's change in countenance and the un-rounding of his shoulders.

The rabbi nods at Elder Cohen. "Maybe you're right. I shall consider the elements of the ketubah – the marriage contract. It is most appropriate to make this decision on Purim — a day of celebration."

"When would you like the betrothal to…" A thunderous sound causes the men to rush toward the front of the house. The rabbi opens the door and closes it quickly.

"It's the Okhrana! They're back!"

"The children – they're in the square," Ivan says.

Chingas runs through the back door, shouting orders to Ivan. "Go through the woods. Get the family to the house. I'll meet you there." Ivan charges into the covering of the woods. Chingas points every cell in his body toward the center of the village, out-distancing the small army of invaders bearing down on horseback. His fears are confirmed as he sees a tiny red-haired boy twirling around the windmill, whipping his stick-sword through the air, his cape flapping around him. The lad is unaware of the panicked villagers running toward their homes.

Chingas focuses on speed, something he has always had. On his left Chingas sees two horses peel off toward some small shanties. To his right two others gallop toward the Volga River's tributary waters where women are running after their children. A good twenty meters to his left another horse parallels Chingas, bent toward the windmill. Chingas locks his vision onto the toddler.

"Faster, legs, faster," he commands. His legs obey, and Chingas picks up speed. He can almost hear his grandson singing, "It's Purim day; It's Purim day." Chingas has no breath to shout. The soldier draws his gun, aiming at his grandson. Tears rise in Chingas' throat as he stretches in the final meter, scooping up the child fully under his left arm and swinging him onto his chest, placing his own body between his grandson and the bullet. The impact of the bullet stops Chingas in midair, and he tries to set Otto down gently as he falls, but he throws the toddler hard. Otto looks surprised and cries.

"Otto, run home, honey. Run now, Otto," Chingas gasps, but Otto just sobs.

"Where's my sword?" the toddler bawls, wiggling away from Chingas.

Chingas knows he's laying on Otto's sword, but he's helpless to move. The red pool around Chingas spreads. The soldier reloads his gun calmly. Chingas fights against a sea of blackness that's pulling him down.

"Otto," Chingas barks. "Otto, go home now! Run!"

Otto looks down at his grandfather and cries louder.

Chingas sees the soldier leveling his gun at the lad. With all his might he throws his body as far in the direction of Otto as he can and slaps him down. The impact of the ball against his forehead knocks Chingas flat. He cannot see. Otto's crying fades. Chingas yields to the darkness.

In the house, Fedora and Galayna bend over the opening in the floor. "Stay quiet, come what may—bushta-budah," Fedora orders her daughters. She closes the opening and Galayna moves a stool on top of it while Fedora removes her apron and the covering from her head with shaking fingers.

"Mother Galayna," she says. "Say a prayer for me, and make sure our girls stay hidden."

"Aye Fedora," says her mother-in-law. Galayna drops to her knees in prayer.

Fedora runs from the house. "Otto!" she yells. She sees Otto standing small and alone near the windmill, crying hysterically. Above him, on a horse, a soldier points his gun toward her son.

"No!" she screams, lifting her skirt to allow her feet to sprint. "No, don't shoot!"

Fedora ignores the surrounding bedlam and charges toward her son, her auburn hair tumbling out of the pins and bouncing down her back. She raises both fists and hits the gunman's horse. The soldier works to calm his steed and Fedora reaches for Otto.

"Grandfather hurt me," Otto cries.

Fedora scoops him up and races her hands over his short blood-spattered body, confirming that he has no wounds. She glances toward her father-in-law lying in a growing circle of deep red. Blood covers his face from a gaping wound above his ear, and his left leg gushes. She turns toward the soldier, protecting as much of her son as she can with her arms. She sees familiar movement and motions to Ivan to stay back. She sets Otto on the ground and pushes him toward his father. Otto runs to Ivan and Fedora faces the soldier defiantly.

"Who is in charge here?" she demands.

"And who is the beauty I am about to shoot?" he answers coldly.

"I am Fedora Tonovich, daughter of Fyodor Tonovich, martyred protector of Russia's great Tsar Nicholas II."

The soldier's face softens. He pockets his gun, dismounts, and gives a slight bow. "Your father is lauded among Orthodox soldiers. It's a great honor to meet you. But I thought the tsarina took you into the palace when you were orphaned. Why are you in this Jewish village?"

Fedora studies the puffy-faced man with tangled purple nose veins, twenty years her senior, and wearing a black wool jacket with ragged edges.

"What is your business with this village?" she asks.

"The Orthodoxy marked this village for annihilation, madam. You will not be harmed, I assure you."

"You have already harmed me. My father-in-law lies dead at my feet."

"A regrettable mistake. He took the balls for the lad."

Fedora's teeth clench together.

"You have it in your heart to annihilate old men and children? Tsarina Alexandra may have my father sainted for saving her husband. He is a hero to the Orthodoxy. My father would never have participated in vulgarity such as this."

"I follow my orders, madam. The pogroms dictate that meetings are forbidden unless the tsar gives permission. This

14

village has been meeting and has stores of food from our troops."

"There have been no meetings. The only church was burned. The villagers fear meeting. As for stores of food, the village is starving. Sixty bodies are waiting in the coolness of the river until we can dig their graves in the frozen ground. No one has food. May I show you?"

"Sixty dead! That is a goodly number. No, madam, I do not need to see it. The word of the daughter of Fyodor Tonovich is sacred. It's most unfortunate that the tsarina herself believes this village to hold food stores sufficient for our soldiers."

"Ah, I see," says Fedora. "The tsarina cannot be wrong, of course."

"No, the tsarina cannot be wrong, though she is German," he says. "Our holy tsar put her in charge of the government when he left to lead the battle against Germany—the tsarina's homeland. It is by her command that we punish this village. We made a pledge to the tsar that we would obey her commands while he is away."

Fedora reaches out her hand and places it on the soldier's arm. "Please, sir. Can you moderate your soldiers? I feel we can come to terms."

The man places his hand on top of Fedora's and holds it to his lips and kisses it. "Certainly, madam. I shall gather my men and we will continue our discussion."

The soldier remounts and gallops away. Fedora stoops down to examine Chingas, listening for breaths. She rips his pants to expose the gaping leg wound, tears fabric from her skirt and shoves it deep into the pulverized flesh. She rips off another layer and binds it tight. She rises to face the group of soldiers now surrounding her.

The leader orders his men to dismount, and stands proudly to their side. "This woman is Fedora Tonovich, daughter of Fyodor Tonovich, martyred protector of our sacred tsar."

Two of the younger soldiers shrug, but a contemporary of the group's leader hits his chest with his fist, and immediately steps forward to bow before Fedora, his greasy hair almost swiping her face. Fedora extends her hand, which is covered with Chingas's blood, and the soldier faintly kisses it.

"Fedora Tonovich, I am honored," says the elderly man. She sees rotted teeth when he smiles, but his expression is genuine. "You look very much like your father. Your father greatly outranked me, but I was in the detail sent to Japan with the tsar. When the assassin appeared, your father was standing nearest the tsar, and did not hesitate to throw himself in front of our holy leader, himself becoming holy. If not for him, Nicholas II would not be alive. We will always be indebted."

Fedora pushes her shoulders back and tilts her chin. "That is correct," she confirms. "My father gave his life for the tsar, and the tsar personally expressed eternal gratitude to me. So, on behalf of our grateful tsar, I command you to leave my village."

"I don't take orders from a Kovno peasant woman," a young soldier jeers.

The group leader draws his pistol and slaps the young ruffian.

Fedora continues, choosing her words with caution. "The tsar is grateful to me, and with his publicly-expressed gratitude, must protect me, my family, and my village forever."

The puffy-faced leader re-pockets his pistol. "Most assuredly, madam. The tsar will be pleased when he learns that we were able to grant your command. We want nothing more than our tsar to be grateful, as we all are. But the tsar is in Germany, and the tsarina has given us orders. The stores of this village must be commandeered for the troops."

"Yes, of course you must bow to the tsarina's dictates. I will bring you all the challah and gefilte, bread and fish, of the village. You shall report that this village completely surrendered to the tsarina's demands. And, of course, in the name of the tsarina, you must take credit for the dead at the river. It is only appropriate."

The leader bows. "We will camp at the edge of town, near the burned area. You may bring us all the stores of this village, and we will report that Kovno surrendered."

"I shall bring it all at first light," she says.

The men walk their horses toward the charred remains of the synagogue. Fedora drops to her knees and checks the bindings on Chingas.

# CHAPTER 2
## *March 20, 1916*

Amalie carries six more candles up the ladder from the cellar.

"Amalie, I need more light," says Fedora, her bloody hands feeling inside Chingas's knee area.

"We've burned through twelve already," says Amalie, lighting fresh candles and setting them around her mother's surgical area. She removes the faded ones and gathers the melted wax. She lights more candles and sets them near her grandfather's head, where her grandmother and Chana sew on his face.

Her father walks in from outside and brushes his rain-soaked clothing. "I've gathered some very meager food offerings from the villagers," he says. He looks at his comatose father. "How is he?"

"He lost his eye," Grandmother's voice sounds flat.

"I think I can save his leg, but I don't know if it will do him much good," says her mother. "Were you able to gather enough?"

"They have almost nothing. It all fits into the small handcart."

"Did you get the chelev? We are forbidden to eat the fat, but they are not."

"Yes. I got everything except what may be inside the rabbi's house. I did not want to tempt your friends to murder me, so I kept my distance from their encampment."

Amalie convulses as her mother pulls her blood-covered hand from her grandfather's leg and holds up the steel ball. "Got it! Amalie, load your needle with plenty of silk and help me sew up his leg. He has lost too much blood."

"I'm not good at doctor things," says Amalie.

"You have to learn," says her father.

Amalie backs away. "Otto was crying about grandfather when I put him down. Should I check on him?"

"Go ahead, Amalie," Ivan says. "I'll change out the rest of the candles."

Amalie gives him the basket of candles and leaves.

"She doesn't like blood," says Fedora. "Light another candle for me, Ivan."

Ivan picks up a candle and lights it. "Will he live?"

"He will live," says Galayna. "I prayed."

"Thank you, mother Galayna," says Fedora. "Your fears will keep infections away."

"Fedora, your faith in mother's prayers always surprises me," says Ivan, watching her loop a stitch. "You never question anything she says."

"And why should I, my husband. Has she ever been wrong?"

"No, she has not," he says. "Otto was upset?"

Fedora re-threads her needle. "Yes. Not about the soldier, though. He cried because he thought his grandfather was mad at him. We tried to comfort him but he needs your father. I need Amalie to get me the herbs. Could you call her back in? She doesn't like surgery but she's very good at mixing herbs."

Ivan walks to the barn and returns with Amalie. He opens the floor for her and she grabs a candle and descends the steps. She picks up the herb bowl and fills it with dried herbs, opens a jar of goo and pours a few drops on the herbs. She opens another jar and adds smelly, granular moisture to the herb bowl. She mashes it together with a stone and ascends the steps.

"Here you are, mother," Amalie says.

"I'm still stitching," says Fedora. "Take it to Chana."

Chana ties off the last stitch above Chingas's ear. Amalie holds out the herb bowl and Chana dips out a generous amount and works it into the stitches on her grandfather's face.

"I need some of that ointment," says Fedora. Amalie takes the bowl to her mother.

"Chana, what happened today?" Ivan asks. "How did you and Amalie get back home?"

"When Amalie and I met Toppur I told him what you said—that you would hold him responsible for our safety. When the raid came he grabbed both of us and we ran for our house, but a soldier yelled at us to stop. Toppur told us to run and we did, and grandmother hid us under the house. I'm not sure what happened to Toppur."

"I looked back and saw him attack the soldier," says Amalie.

"Toppur was badly beaten," Ivan says.

"Father, I must go to him," says Chana.

"No, you cannot help him. He has serious head injuries—it looks like a broken skull. I doubt that even your mother can help him."

"But I shall try to help Toppur," says Fedora. "Stay focused, Chana. Your grandfather needs your best work."

Chana sniffles.

"There are at least ten others that need your skills," Ivan says.

"I knew there would be needs," Fedora says. "I have to bathe when I finish here, and then I must take the cart to our oppressors so they will leave. It's dangerous to let them linger. It will be daylight before I can help the injured."

"I can help them, mother," offers Chana. "Please."

Fedora watches her daughter's small hands treating the wounds.

"You have the gift, Chana, there is no doubt. But you are too young. You must develop judgment first, my daughter."

"But mother," Chana argues. "May I just go ahead of you and bind the bleeding. I will tell them you are coming. Please mother."

"Are there any wounded that Chana might help?" Fedora asks. "I don't want her to touch anyone that might die. There is too much superstition in the village."

"Yes, there are two that she might help," Ivan says

"Very well, Ivan. When we finish here, you may take our Chana and allow her to administer her gifts." Fedora stretches her neck and back and returns to her work. "And Ivan, tell those who bleed to apply steady pressure on top of the wounds. The bleeding must be stopped."

"They won't. They fear touching death."

"Tell them anyway. Remind them that they can be cleansed if they touch death, but that the dead have no such opportunity."

"What about Toppur?" Chana asks.

"You cannot go to him," Fedora says. "I'll get to him as quickly as I can."

"There, my dearest, you are mended," says Galayna to her husband. "Let's move him to the floor. I don't want him to thrash and fall off the table."

Amalie rolls out her grandparents' sleeping mat on the floor. The three adults and two young women carefully lower the family's patriarch to the mat and Galayna covers him with a quilt.

Fedora and Galayna pick up one end of the table and Ivan picks up the other and they return it to the back-porch area. The two women wash it thoroughly, while the Chana and Amalie scrub the floor. When they finish the two women walk into the black rain to the tributary to bathe. Chana and Amalie clean the surgical instruments and wrap them in cloth.

"I'm ready, Father," Chana says.

"Amalie, you mind the candles, then put yourself to bed. Come, my little doctor. I shall take you to the Rosen's. Mrs. Rosen was shot in the shoulder, and some of the fragments wounded her baby."

"Aha," says Chana as she disappears into the night with her father.

Amalie stands quietly among the bright candles, trying not to look at her grandfather. She pinches out the candles one by one, taking her time to study the dancing flames. As the room darkens she cries. Her sniffles and tears continue as she wraps the warm waxy stubs in bark paper and carries the last candle to the doorway. She changes into her nightdress and walks to the barn, where her little brother, Otto, snores softly. Amalie slips into bed beside him and places her arm around her sleeping brother.

"I have a wonderful Purim story," she whispers. "There was once a beautiful queen named Fedora. She saved a village, with help from her brave and bold father." Her trickling tears feel hot as they cross her face. Soon she is asleep.

For four days Galayna refuses to eat as she watches over Chingas, moistening his lips and mouth and praying. On the fifth day he stirs. She wipes his lips with a damp cloth.

"What day is it?" Chingas croaks.

"Purim was almost a week ago," says Galayna, her chin quivering.

Chingas moves his head toward her voice. "Purim? Oh no! Otto! My baby boy!" Chingas wails.

"Hush hush now. He is fine," Galayna says.

"He is?"

"Yes. We are all fine – except you. Husband, you were shot twice – once in the leg, and once in the…" her voice catches and she clears her throat. "…once in the face. You lost your eye."

Chingas's hand feels his bandaged face. A smile turns up the corners of his mouth. "Are we not blessed? It was your prayers, Galayna."

Galayna moves his head to see if his ear is damaged. "Old man, you were shot in the face," she shouts into his ear.

"I heard you the first time," he retorts, slapping toward her. "Probably improve my looks," he says, struggling to move. "Help me get up."

"Not today. Fedora wants you to eat first. Your leg is broken. It took her four hours to remove the bullets and put you back together. She will need to splint it before you try to move."

Chingas falls back down. "All right," he says. "Maybe tomorrow." He is quiet for several seconds. "Did I miss the whiskey?"

"No, my husband. Fedora poured it into you during the surgery."

"Ha! So, the whiskey is all gone, I had it all, and I don't remember it. Same as Purim last year."

# CHAPTER 3
## *May 1916*

Ivan sinks his shovel into the garden's dirt and Fedora follows him with potato seeds.

"You shovel needs sharpening," says Fedora.

"Every time I sharpen it, it gets smaller," says Ivan.

For three weeks Ivan has used his shovel every day, burying those who died over the past winter. He had known all of them while they breathed. In death they looked clay-like, particularly those who had spent most of the winter tethered to the river's dock. Few men could help dig. The rabbi was there every day, digging, lifting, dropping, shoveling, covering, tapping. Those without shovels borrowed from the dead or used their axes and knives to carve memory sticks, hammering them into the ground for each grave. The task was too great for such a small force and they ended up placing family members together in a single grave. They began the project shortly after the Okhrana raid and it continued until last week. Every morning at sunrise Ivan went to the grave site and worked until the sun disappeared. Now, completely drenched in death, he is surprised that no one has shunned him. It is disgraceful to use his grave-shovel to plant life in the garden, but no one cares. The old ways are disappearing. Death is too common.

Yesterday he had to bury two strangers with his shovel—refugees from Siberia. Rabbi Wecht brought them in the morning and Fedora administered care, but they died before noon and were buried in a common grave with no marker.

The tsar has begun closing the prison camps in Siberia, reassigning the guards to the central government. Rumor has it that the soldiers caught a night train and when the prisoners awoke, the gates were open and their wardens were gone. A few prisoners managed to board south-bound trains, but they have been offloaded randomly. For the past three days Rabbi Wecht has picked up Siberian refugees from the train station and brought them to Kovno. Fedora was chosen to treat them. Ivan has watched her give tender care but there is no food.

Yesterday Fedora split one of the seed potatoes between their three children. Ivan's parents, Chingas and Galayna, arose early this morning to hunt for edibles in the forest. The forest is full of unsavory villains. His father is still recovering from being shot on Purim day, but both his parents assured him they would be all right.

Four refugees stay in the barn, two men and a woman with her baby. Fedora and Ivan had to move their three children, Chana, Amalie, and Otto, to the damp back porch. Ivan shakes his head.

Toppur's piercing screeches draw Ivan's attention. Fedora rises to her feet and joins her husband.

"It looks like Rabbi Wecht is bringing another refugee," Ivan says.

"Toppur is certainly upset," says Fedora, taking his shovel.

Fedora rests the shovel against her breast and uses the back of her wrist to move sweaty hair away from her face. Her ragged work dress hangs limp over her bony frame. She shields her eyes with a stained hand, peering into the morning sun toward commotion coming from the main part of Kovno. Toppur, suffering brain injuries from the beatings he took on Purim, darts hysterically around Rabbi Wecht, who is helping a feeble woman.

"Death woman! Death woman!" Toppur screams, pointing at the refugee woman.

"What is the cause of Toppur's madness?" Ivan asks.

Fedora brushes off her hands. "Toppur's screams are my envy, husband," she admits. "This woman is our fifth refugee."

"Are you all right?" Ivan asks.

"I'm thinking about the seed potato I fed to the children last evening. They needed the nourishment. These refugees—I can clean them and bind their wounds, but we can't feed them."

Ivan removes his tattered brimmed hat to wipe his forehead on his sleeve. His sweat-matted black hair glints in the sun. He replaces the hat and hastens to help Rabbi Wecht.

Fedora looks around at her freshly-planted rows. "Grow faster," she says. She picks up the shovel and follows her husband towards the bizarre trio.

"Death woman! Death woman!" Toppur rants, spasmodically lurching through the air around the Rabbi and the decrepit woman.

"Toppur, my friend," soothes Fedora as she approaches. "Toppur, look at me. Toppur, it's all right, child. She is yet alive, Toppur—see her trying to walk?"

Toppur's wild eyes won't focus on Fedora and he continues his ear-splitting repetition, "Death woman! Death woman," dodging Fedora's outstretched hand.

"It's no use," pants Rabbi Wecht, stopping to balance the woman upright. He waits until Toppur dashes in front again, and barks, "Toppur go home!" Immediately Toppur howls as if scalded, and runs off shrieking.

Ivan approaches the pathetic refugee and places his arm around her to encourage her forward. The woman collapses against him. Fedora observes that the rabbi allows Ivan to assume the entire load. The rabbi is carrying a bucket, and Fedora guesses the contents – more rancid fat. Ivan's strength has been waning over recent weeks, and the load, albeit thin, will tax him.

"Ivan," says the rabbi, "I was hoping the conclusion of the Bolshevik revolution would bring an end to starvation," he says, "but now, with all the trainloads of political prisoners leaving Siberia…" He doesn't complete the thought. "I know your barn is full, Ivan, but I just could not leave this woman to die."

The load against Ivan sags, and he adjusts the woman against his side and places her arm around his neck, bracing her firmly. "It's all right, Rabbi," Ivan concedes. "It looks like we have another guest, Fedora."

Fedora meets his black eyes with her blue ones, searching for reassurance, but she only sees resignation. She turns and kicks the sides of her skirt to allow her feet to move more freely, and bows her neck homeward.

Fedora sets the shovel inside the barn and stands there in the dim morning light. There is Dagmar, a refugee from one of the rabbi's previous calls, trying to nurse her baby. Fedora hopes the baby will latch but doubts it has the strength. Even if it did, Dagmar's body will likely give no suck. The infant cannot thrive. Fedora sees that the other refugees have given Dagmar and her baby the preferred corner in the barn. Fedora rubs her hands in some straw and uses the skirt of her dress to wipe sweat from her face. Tonight, a single loaf of hard bread must serve one additional mouth, unless Ivan's parents succeed in their search for food among the forest's vegetation.

Fedora rearranges her scarf, brushes her skirt, nods encouragement to Dagmar and strides toward the house.

Ivan and Rabbi Wecht approach the back porch. Fedora points to an empty stool, and Ivan balances the breathing skeleton on it. Fedora stares at the lethargic woman.

"Don't worry, Fedora," says Rabbi Wecht. "The outcome is not in your hands." He sets his bucket on the table.

"More fat?" asks Ivan.

"Aye. More fat. Not edible, of course, but fit for candles and soap."

"Thank you, Rabbi," says Fedora. She removes it from her table and opens the back door and calls inside the house. "Chana, Amalie. We have a newcomer. Come quickly." She turns back to Ivan. "You and Rabbi go over to the lye bin and rid your clothing of vermin. Use the ashes on your arms and around your necks as well."

Fedora covers the table and sets out scraping instruments and folded washcloths. She places a large pot of water on the fire. She looks at the curtained-off corner of the porch where her children sleep, cuddling together for warmth. Each night she secures their quilts and gives thanks for the roof. Sometimes, like last night, Otto sneaks into the house, steps over his sleeping grandparents, climbs the ladder, and snuggles between his parents. He was still sleeping when she and Ivan arose to work in the garden. She looks at the barn. Where will this newcomer sleep?

Fedora steps inside to check on the children. Chana and Amalie, wearing their work dresses, have their black hair tied in rounded braids on top of their heads. Amalie forces Otto's arms into a shirt.

"We know our duty, mother," says Chana. Chana opens the trap door in the floor and drops down to get the root medicines and soap. Amalie rolls up her sleeves and gets the comb from the bureau.

"Amalie, I can help," pesters Otto. Amalie purses her lips and walks to the back porch with her mother, Otto at her heels. When Otto breaks through the back door he runs past Ivan, who scoops up the toddler and tosses him onto his back. Otto squeals and laughs.

"Keep him with you," says Fedora. "Our work will require our full attention."


Ivan and Rabbi Wecht watch the three women convert the porch dining area into a hospital.

"Ivan, isn't it about time you tell me how you and Fedora met?" asks the rabbi.

"Perhaps," says Ivan.

"Of course, you were smitten by her beauty," says the rabbi.

"I was," says Ivan.

"Why would such a beauty choose you?" asks the rabbi.

"It was my day of good fortune," says Ivan. "I fear she stilted her spirit by marrying me."

"Where else would her medical gifts be so needed?" asks the rabbi. "This gentile wife of yours, Ivan – she is matchless. I depend on Fedora's gift of healing, as do the villagers, whether they admit it or not. Your little Chana is also a gifted healer."

"Fedora says that Chana could deliver a baby by herself if needed."

"You still haven't answered my question about meeting and marrying a gentile," says Rabbi Wecht. "One of these days you will tell me the story."

"Of course," says Ivan. "Walk with me, Rabbi. The women need privacy to do their work."


Fedora sees the men disappear around the corner of the barn and motions to her daughters, who remove the rags from the woman's emaciated filthy body. Fedora lifts the heavy pot of hot water from the fire and pours it into a large tub. Amalie adds an appropriate amount of cold water from the barrel, and Chana encourages the newcomer toward the water, but the woman only stares. Fedora and Chana each take an arm and assist the woman into the tub. She sits in the water and Chana pours a small pitcher of water slowly over the woman's head.

Amalie retrieves the metal laundry pail from the wall and places it on the ground, away from the main work area. She lowers a bucket into the water barrel, lugs it to the metal laundry pail, and dumps it in. She drops in a measure of white powdered lye and watches the water heat. She picks up the woman's clothing with a stick, throws it into the lye mixture, and stirs.

Fedora and Chana examine the listless woman's body. For the next hour or so they delouse, scrape, probe, pick and comb the filth and organisms away from infested flesh.

"All right, you are clean," decrees Fedora to the living corpse. "You must sit over there on the stool so we can rinse you one last time. Can you help us? Come, my dear, use your legs. That's right. Let's walk to the stool. It's time to heal." The woman slumps her bones on the stool. Amalie and Chana work together to re-fill the bucket with warm water. They slowly pour it over the woman while Fedora wipes, punctures and purges.

After the final rinsing Amalie drags the tub of bath water to the hillside and turns it on its edge, watching it make small streamlets. She places the empty tub next to the soaking rags and breaks off some bar soap for laundering. She uses her stick to transfer the rags from the lye mixture to the tub.

"I'm going to the river," she announces. "I'm pretty sure her clothes will disintegrate, but I'll try to keep them intact." With that she drags the tub downhill toward a ditch that leads to the river.

Fedora studies a sore on the woman's shoulder. "Chana, do you have the roots?"

"Yes, mother." Chana removes some salve from the jar, and passes it to her mother. After they finish applying the crushed medications to the more obvious places, they commence their inspection. Chana begins from the feet, and Fedora from the head. Fedora examines the stupefied woman. She walks her fingers around the cleansed blond scalp and peers inside her ears and passive blue-gray eyes. She opens the woman's mouth and leans her head back. Her back molars are large and new, and the woman's teeth are intact, which is unusual for a refugee. She closes the mouth and pulls at skin around the eyes and cheeks. The woman is in her mid-twenties – something Fedora would not have guessed. Fedora moves her critical eyes down the white body, medicating generously. She sees faded evidence of childbearing across the woman's belly. Fedora gently touches the white streaks, recalling stories about the cruelties Siberia played on the babies and their forlorn mothers.

"This woman has suffered more than others," says Fedora.

"I think she might be pretty," says Chana. "Where shall I lay her?"

"We have no mats or blankets," says Fedora.

"She can have my bed," says Chana. "Amalie and I will share." Chana leads the woman to her bed and bids her down. She prepares a watered herb tea, and pours it into a cup over a crust of bread. Fedora watches her daughter offer the cup of nourishment to the newcomer. Chana sits on her knees in front of the mute woman.

"Please, madam. Please eat," Chana begs. The woman lifts her round pale eyes and stares blankly at Chana. "I want her to live, mother."

"I know, Chana, but I can offer you no hope," Fedora says. "If she wants to die we will provide her with a comfortable grave."

"Please, madam. Please, just drink a little," Chana begs. When the vacant eyes don't respond, Chana cries.

Fedora walks over and kneels beside her daughter. "Chana, Chana, Chana. You are becoming wise in healing bodies, but you have much to learn about wills. If this woman's will has been destroyed, she has already sent her soul to God, and no matter how long you spoon food into her, her body will not live. But you watch – if there is a spark of her will left, she'll feed herself and perhaps she can begin to heal. You must let it be, my daughter. It's between her and God now. Set down the cup."

Chana sniffles and wipes her eyes. "Is it all right if I just put the cup into her hands?"

"No," Fedora says.

Chana looks into the woman's face. "Please, madam. Please live," she begs. The woman's cold translucent fingers wrap around the cup. She moves the cup to her lips and swallows. Chana smiles. The woman returns the half empty cup to Chana and Chana helps her lay down. She covers the naked body with a blanket and closes the curtain.

Fedora cleans the instruments and scrubs the table and benches. Chana runs to help Amalie, who is dragging the tub of clean rags up the hill. The young women clean the containers and return them to their places. When order is restored, Fedora tells her daughters to gather ingredients for one loaf of bread. Amalie disappears into the cabin's trap door with a candle.

"How is the supply of dried potato skins?" Fedora asks Amalie.

"I'm scraping bottom," Amalie calls. "Perhaps we have enough to grind up for a few more loaves."

"Chana, keep the fire going just long enough to bake one small loaf. Amalie, you will need to render the fat that the rabbi brought. We have enough candles for the summer months. Make it into soap. You will need to share the fire. Our wood is low."

"Aye, mother," they both reply.

Fedora shades her eyes and looks toward the garden. Two of their stronger refugees have joined Ivan and the rabbi in removing weeds. Caring for the garden is a priority, and the weeds steal precious nutrients from the soil. She walks to the barn to fetch the hoe, and joins the weeding party.


AFTER A FEW hours loosening weeds and turning soil, Fedora spots Franco, their healthiest refugee guest, weeding his way toward her until he is four rows away. Fedora knows Franco must talk—it's part of the healing process, and Franco has progressed almost enough to continue his journey forward. Talking openly is a healthy symptom but she has heard sickening stories about Siberia and doesn't wish to hear more.

32

"Work is a blessing," comments Franco. "That woman that the rabbi brought in? 'Death woman' the idiot called her."

"Can you help me get this noxious weed, Franco?" Fedora asks. "You seem to know about gardens. Did you have garden work in Siberia?"

"No. I was on the fence-building detail – wire fences with barbs. Once inside the fence, our only work was living. Even when sick we knew we had to stay on our feet and keep moving. I stayed alive two winters. No one made it through three."

"Be careful, Franco. That area is planted. Watch the rows."

"I wasn't in the worst camp," Franco says. "The worst camp was fifty kilometers north. There was a witch there—a lot of people tried to kill her, but she wouldn't die. Everyone who touched her caught the plague. Even the guards kept their distance. She was a pretty blond woman, with eyes like a wolf."

"Be careful not to pull up the vegetable, Franco."

"Two months ago, the witch blew up her whole camp—we felt the earth shake. They knew she did it but they couldn't catch her. If she got to the south-bound train she would be arriving about now. That woman—Death Woman—I think she's the witch."

"We don't allow rumors, Franco."

"Death woman," he repeats. "That explosion caused the closure of a lot of Siberian prisons. Even the tsar fears her."

Regardless of Franco's needs, Fedora cannot listen any longer. She motions for Ivan. "You are right, Franco," she says, stretching her back. "Work is a blessing. It helps me forget how hungry I am. I must check on our supper. Enjoy the work, my friend. Here, you may use the hoe. Put it in the barn when you finish." Ivan joins her and they both step over the rows until they reach the last. They stop and gaze toward the forest, looking for movement.

"They should have been back by now," Ivan says. "They left very early. Carrying those large baskets, anyone could see that they're looking for food. Their foraging mission is dangerous, with all the forest marauders."

"Aye, my husband, but they are wiser than foxes. They want to bring something for us to put in the boiling water, and you know your father – he will not return until he succeeds. They are stronger than you think. And your mother's God protects them. They are fine."

"You're probably right. Worrying isn't helpful." Ivan walks to the water bucket and dips in the ladle and drinks freely, letting it spill over his face.

"Ivan. Look. Here they come!" Fedora lifts her skirt and jaunts toward the tree line, anxious to see what her in-laws found. Galayna waves, a sure sign of success. When Fedora reaches Galayna the two women drop to their knees to delve into the baskets.

"Oh, wonderful!" Fedora exclaims, holding up a mushroom.

"We had to travel almost to Guerns for the wild onions, but look at the size," says Chingas. "We found six bird eggs, and I was wishing I could climb trees like Otto. I was certain there were eggs but the limbs were too high for us." The patch over his eye is slightly askew and Fedora examines the healing.

"You look a little pale," Fedora says. "Did you stay warm enough?"

"Of course he didn't," says Galayna. "He leaned heavily on his walking stick and kept both his sweaters on all day."

"I can't take off my sweaters or you'll wash them," says Chingas. "You don't have to fuss, Fedora. My hat kept me warm enough."

Fedora hugs him. "You're our family protector, dearest father," she says. "I'd give you my sweater if it fit you."

"As would I," says Galayna.

"It's a wonder I can heal with all this pampering," says Chingas.

"Come let's go to the kitchen before our curious guests join us," says Ivan, closing up the baskets.

Chana and Amalie greet their grandparents as the four adults approach the porch. Fedora and Galayna spread out the harvest on the kitchen table.

"Oh my!" exclaims Amalie. "You found onions!"

"And eggs," Chana adds, touching the small blue rounds.

"And a basket of bark for bread," says Galayna.

Chingas gulps a ladle of water and dips another, offering it to Galayna. Galayna drinks a little, and Chingas finishes it. He picks up the barrel and pours the remaining water into the bucket and rolls the huge drum toward the river to refill. The community well is in the middle of town, but a fresh creek runs much closer. On his way, Chingas motions to Franco. Franco drops the hoe and skips carefully over the rows.

"Amalie, go get the hoe Franco dropped," says Fedora. "Clean it and put it in the barn."

Ivan picks up the axe and splits wood to stoke the fire.

"I believe it is enough for three or four days," declares Galayna. The women divide the spoils into four piles, handling the tiny eggs with care.

"The soup will be very tasty," says Fedora kissing her mother-in-law's cheek. "With your blessing on it, Dagmar will even have suck for her baby."

Fedora puts the kettle on the fire and glances around for her red-haired toddler. Otto would generally have his nose in the middle of things. It's been too long since she's seen him. "Ivan, have you seen Otto?" she calls.

Ivan rises from splitting wood, looks around for his son.

"There he is, behind the barn," Ivan answers pointing. Fedora follows the direction of his finger and spies Otto walking carefully, holding up the front of his shirt and studying whatever he has tucked into it. Fedora hopes it isn't harmful. She, Galayna and Ivan set down their work and walk toward him.

"What do you have there, son?" asks Ivan.

Otto looks up at his parents. He looks down at the contents of his shirt, and back up at his father, his blue eyes round with wonder. His mother and grandmother bend over him to inspect.

"Oh my!" says Galayna.

"Why, Otto!" exclaims Ivan. "It's a grouse's nest." The boy's chubby hands hang on to the nest as Ivan carefully lifts it from his shirt. He shows the contents to Fedora.

"You poor little babies!" she whispers as she gazes at the featherless creatures, craning their peeping faces upward in search of food. To Ivan's surprise, Fedora weeps. She takes the nest from Ivan, cradles it in her arms and sits on the ground, sobbing. Chingas joins them. The three adults and little boy stand quietly while Fedora cries.

"Son," Fedora says tearfully. "These babies are like everyone else here. But they are luckier..." Her voice breaks. "They are luckier because they eat bugs and worms, and we have plenty of those," she giggles nervously through her tears. "Perhaps your grandfather can help you tend them."

"Aye," says Chingas. He helps Fedora return the nest to Otto's shirt, puts his arm around the toddler, and walks him toward the garden area.

"Bugs and worms," he says to Otto as they walk. "Did I ever tell you the story of how the bugs used to eat the birds? That was before the birds decided to grow bigger than the bugs..."

# CHAPTER 4
## *Summer 1916*

Fedora walks toward the house after bathing off the garden grit, raking back her wet hair with her fingers. To her right is the fruit of her day's labor, a growing crop of healthy vegetables rising to the bright afternoon sun. Otto's four birds run behind him near the barn, providing entertainment and distraction from starvation for her family and guests. Fedora hurries into the house and closes the door behind her. She descends through the hatch and fishes through her empty larder, hoping for a vegetable, and finds a shriveled potato for today's soup. She carries it outside to the kitchen area, and decides to thin the beets and carrots again. She sees Franco hurrying toward her.

"Mrs. Meinrel. Look!" Franco says, opening his hand excitedly.

"A green bean!" exclaims Fedora. "Our first green bean. Oh, Franco! Look, girls. Our first harvest!"

Amalie and Chana jump around in delight.

"Franco, I will chop it small enough so that each bowl has a piece. You may announce it after prayer. Could you carefully thin the greens again? Break off every fourth beet green. We only need a handful."

"Yes, mam."

The fervor of the first harvest creates a festive mood as the Meinrels and their guests enjoy their soup and bark bread around the outdoor table.

"Please excuse me," says Dagmar. "I must check on my baby."

Fedora prepares a bowl of soup and bread for the mute woman in Chana's bed.

"I'll give it to her, mother," says Chana. "She walked again today, to the barn and back. She likes Dagmar's baby." Chana sits beside the woman, extending the bowl.

"It's a green bean, Miss," Chana explains to the hollow gray eyes. "It's from our garden." Chana leaves the soup in the woman's hands.

"Well done, Chana," says Fedora. They return to the dinner table.

"Mrs. Meinrel!" calls Dagmar. "There's a soldier at the road. He looks like he might be coming here." Fedora pales as she glances nervously toward the garden where premature vegetation dances too largely in the evening sun. Ivan and Chingas walk to the road.

"Everyone, please, continue with your meal and remain calm," Fedora encourages, and she runs to catch up with the men.

"Greetings, sir," says Chingas.

"I see that you are eating. I'm sorry to disturb you," says the soldier, removing his hat.

The man is about thirty and wears the brown uniform of the Bolshevik rebels. He has a large black mustache, generous sideburns and thick black hair. He's a couple inches shorter than Ivan and hasn't been touched with starvation, although he isn't overweight. His dark brown eyes appear too soft for an officer in the rebel army, and when he speaks his voice is kind. The officer gives a slight bow to Fedora. Amalie joins them, standing behind Chingas.

"Hello, sirs, madam, miss. I am Yosef Roseman." Yosef holds his hat tightly against his chest, twisting it. "I understand that Fanya Kaplan might be here."

"No, I don't know anyone by that name, sir," answers Ivan. Yosef's eyes sadden.

"Mr. Roseman. Perhaps you could describe her. If we see her, we can notify you," offers Fedora.

"No, but thank you, madam. I will continue my search. I was hoping she would be here. So many people know of your hospitality. I thought if she survived, she might have made her way here."

"Please, sir, join us for dinner," Fedora says. "We have some soup and a little bread we can share."

"No, not today. But I brought you something. Some flour. When I offered it to the rabbi, he said to bring it directly here. It's in a barrel in my wagon."

"Flour! You brought us flour?" asks Fedora. She rushes the three men to the wagon, and supervises the unloading of the barrel, directing them toward the house.

The refugees see the approaching uniform and scatter to the barn.

"Do not give them reassurance, and do not mention this flour," she instructs.

"I don't understand," says Amalie who is walking with her mother.

"They must prepare their minds for leaving," explains Fedora. "Just as the mother eagle places sharp sticks in the nest to encourage her babies to fly, so we must make things uncomfortable enough to help them progress on their journey."

Fedora motions for the men to roll the barrel inside the house. She closes the door behind them and lifts the trap door. The three men lower the barrel through the opening, close up the floor and follow Fedora outside.

"Mr. Roseman," Fedora smiles. "I wish you would reconsider. We have the first of our harvest today, and we are celebrating."

"No, madam. You are feeding enough."

"Thank you for the gift, Mr. Roseman. I assure you we will put it to good use. Will you return another time and share dinner?"

"No, I must continue my quest. Your neighbor said that the rabbi brought a blond woman here, and I was hoping it was my Fanya. I am sorry to have bothered you." The soldier gives a courteous bow and turns on his heel before Fedora can respond.

As he turns, Yosef Roseman freezes in place. In front of him, leaning against Chana, is their mute patient, Fanya Kaplan. The Meinrels have not known her name until this minute. Fedora can see Fanya's passive expression and wonders if she will acknowledge this man who obviously loves her.

Yosef Roseman's rigid stance relaxes. He steps to Fanya, brings her gently into his arms and kisses her face. His shoulders shake. He holds Fanya back and looks at her. Fanya raises thin fingers and brushes moisture from his eyes, leans her face into his and kisses him.

# CHAPTER 5
## *1917*

Frequent visits from Yosef, along with generous gifts of food and clothing, have helped the Meinrel family survive the winter of 1916-17. Now the muddy garden waits for potato seeds as Ivan breaks up clumps of dirt. Fedora works nearby.

"Ivan, look at Fanya," says Fedora. "Yosef is taking her for a walk along the river."

"I don't think she's strong enough for such a walk," he says, stretching his back.

"I worry less about the walk than the talk," says Fedora.

"Yosef will do all the talking," says Ivan. "He has high hopes for her."

"I know. He thinks she responds but he doesn't notice that she never talks," says Fedora.

"He loves her. He cannot go a week without seeing her, even if he must travel several hours. That type of devotion is rare," says Ivan. "I've heard her talk."

"She only gives occasional one-word answers," says Fedora. "Her emotions are not intact. She holds onto deep suffering."

"I wish we knew more about what she went through," Ivan says. "She looks so—haunted. Yosef doesn't see it."

"Aye, that is the worry," says Fedora. "He thinks she's still the same woman he once loved."

"Yosef says he can be here through the fall. Perhaps all the attention will help her."

"She has a long path ahead."

"It looks like she has someone who wants to walk it with her," says Ivan, returning to his labors.


Throughout the summer the crops respond to the constant care of the Meinrels, producing a favorable harvest.

In the fall, the Meinrel's carry their harvest of winter squash, beets, potatoes and onions to the cellar beneath their house.

Fanya sits on the porch bench weaving a needle in and out of a quilt as the Meinrel's go back and forth between the garden and the house. She thinks about Siberia. For ten years she survived unspeakable horrors in that death camp. The best and worst part of her imprisonment was her baby daughter, born a few months after she arrived in camp. The delivery was difficult. Even during labor they hadn't spared her from abuse. Miraculously baby Zoë survived and provided Fanya's body and spirit with warmth she had never known. Many of Yosef's expressions remind her of Zoë.


ZOË HAD A MOP of black hair, like Yosef's—straight and wild, adding to her enchanting expressions. There was never enough food to provide adequate suck for Zoë, but Fanya's strength overpowered other prisoners and she developed skills to insure Zoë's survival, sometimes surprising herself with her abilities. Even the guards feared her. In the end it wasn't enough.

Shortly after Zoë's first birthday Fanya became ill and her milk dried up. It was late fall, like today. Fanya tried to ingest the tainted food but she couldn't keep it in. When she fed it to Zoë, it made the baby sick. Zoë had cried until she was too weak. Her tiny face and body thinned and her dark eyes grew large with confusion. Fanya helplessly watched her daughter die, soothing her tears during the long process.

If Zoë had died in the summer, a grave could have been dug, but burying her in a snowdrift just brought the wolves. She shudders as she remembers the blood against the white barren ground, and the fragments of hair and clothing.


FANYA'S NEEDLE FLIES wildly out of the quilt and jabs her finger. She watches her blood ooze onto her work.

No, she will not tell Yosef Roseman of his daughter. He would want to know everything, and she cannot say it.

As usual, Yosef shows up shortly before supper, this time driving a small wagon pulled by an aging mare. Chingas Meinrel leaves his harvesting chores and limps to greet his young friend, extending a calloused handshake.

"Yosef. Welcome. You're just in time for supper – you must join us."

"Thank you, Chingas," says Yosef. "I seem to be here so often that I could be one of your refugees."

"You have been overly generous, Yosef," corrects Chingas. "Flour is precious, and you have given us enough to get us through the winter again."

"Is young Otto in the house? I have a gift for him."

"The women sent him on a tree-climbing errand. They didn't want him to know that they're boiling one of his birds. My eye is not as sharp as yours, but if you look toward the woods you will probably see him. He has determined to climb every tree in the forest."

"Yes, I see him. Thanks. Could you take this package to Fedora? It's coats for your women and Fanya." Chingas takes the package and Yosef walks toward the trees and shouts for Otto. When Otto, now five, turns and sees Yosef, he jumps down from a tree and sets his short legs in motion, knowing Yosef brought him another gift. Instead of running to the wagon as he usually does, the lad runs right into Yosef and throws his arms around his legs. Yosef bends down and hugs the boy, then picks him up and carries him back to the wagon.

"Chickens!" shouts Otto gleefully.

"Not chickens, Otto. Hens. Egg-laying hens. And feed for them."

"Dad! I have hens!" yells, breaking from Yosef and running to the garden. Dagmar, with her baby strapped to her back, picks Otto up by the back of the breeches before he tramples too many vegetables and gently tosses him toward his father.

After sharing a meal with their many guests in the outdoor eating area, the family retires inside with Fanya and Yosef. The room has three pieces of furniture: two small stools and a bureau. Chingas and Galayna sit on stools, and Galayna lights the lantern on the bureau while Fanya and Yosef, Fedora and Ivan, and the children seat themselves on the floor. Otto, who is not generally allowed inside with guests, sneaks in next to Amalie. The group is closely spaced, with only a small gap forming the middle of the room.

"Aye," says Chingas resting his elbows on his knees.

"No talking politics," Galayna warns him.

"Who, me? No, of course not," he says, scratching his chin. "But we must all accept that there will now be an end to the tsars of Russia."

"Bah, there you go!" says Galayna, waving her hand at him.

"I'm talking history, not politics," Chingas defends. "After four centuries, no more tsars. It feels unnatural not to be targeted for persecution."

"The harsh era of a ruling family is finally ended," says Yosef. "It is the dawn of socialism, where workers will guide the country. We shall work together for the good of each other. The workers are in charge."

"I just do not feel as in charge of the country as the new leaders say that I am," says Chingas.

"But you will, Father," says Ivan. "You will feel in charge. The pogroms are over. There are many Jews in high government offices. We may even be allowed to return to our Hebrew customs."

"It's been so long, I barely remember them," says Galayna.

"Aye, you have been a stubborn one through it all," says Chingas. "You kept up the faith until the rabbi ordered you to stop because you were endangering the entire village."

"Our heritage is not to be trifled with – not even by a tsar," Galayna says, spitting on the floor. "Each week, each month, each holiday, we said, 'maybe next year.' It's been thirty years! An entire generation has missed the beauty of our heritage."

"Lenin says that the workers will decide all of the laws," offers Yosef.

Fedora clenches her hands. "But what of the tsar and his lovely family? What will happen to them?"

"They will live in the winter palace and work alongside the new government to assure a smooth transition," says Yosef. "Ultimately they will live in a different country. The tsarina wishes to live in Germany, of course, but I doubt the family can go there since we're still warring with that country."

"A lot of people blame Tsar Nicholas II," says Ivan. "So many died from his brutality—even people here in Kovno."

"Yes, but the tsar was the first to say he wasn't ready to be our tsar," says Yosef.

"The Bolsheviks want the tsar executed," says Ivan.

"No, that is just a rumor," says Yosef. "Vladimir Lenin has assured their safety, and he is overseeing this new regime. Fanya and Lenin were revolutionaries together—they are comrades. Fanya, tell them how Vladimir Lenin will protect the tsar's family."

"He will have them shot," states Fanya.

Fedora gasps and grabs her stomach. "Chana, Amalie," she says. "Help your brother wash and prepare for bed."

"Nooo!" whimpers Otto, trying to back further into the wall. Chana and Amalie help him to his feet, and the three children trudge away.

"Yosef, do you have a family?" Chingas asks.

"My father was a professor at the university in St. Petersburg. He died before I finished my education, but he provided well for me."

"What about your parents, Fanya?" Galayna asks.

Fanya folds her arms around her legs, gazes at her knees and rocks back and forth. The silence grows uncomfortable.

"Yosef," solicits Ivan. "How did you and Fanya meet?"

Yosef smiles at Fanya and she relaxes her grip around her knees. "I'll have to tell my version," responds Yosef. "She will have a different recollection, for sure."

"It was more than ten years ago – August 30, 1905 to be exact. I was late for a lecture in St. Petersburg, and I slipped into the back of the hall. On the bench in front of me and slightly to my right was Fanya. Her blond hair was long and full—down to the bench. She was wearing a fur coat that she was trying to shed, and I moved behind her and helped her remove it.

"Her brown dress had about thirty buttons down the back. I leaned a little closer to try to see her face when the speaker said something that upset her and she abruptly stood to impugn him. I almost fell across her bench." Yosef laughs. "The speaker totally ignored her so, what does my Fanya do? She jumps onto the bench, trying to balance herself on top of her fur coat. Her voice rang so clearly through the air, but her feet were slipping around so I stood behind her and, nervous as I was, placed my hands around her waist to help her balance. Her waist was tiny— my fingers almost touched. Her body was trembling, but I was the only one who knew it. She was fearless."

"What did the speaker say that upset Fanya?" asks Ivan.

"I have no idea," Yosef says. "But I could tell that she was relying on my hands to keep her steady. She raised both her arms straight up in the air and I looked up at her face. I've never seen anything so alive. I loved her. Then others began joining her chant. I watched her enliven the entire room. The police came and I literally had to carry her away to protect her."

Fedora watches Fanya for signs of emotion. Fanya knows she must say something, but her gaze fixes on her twisting hands.

"I tried not to love him," Fanya finally says, her eyes darting.

Fedora touches Fanya's hand and addresses Yosef, keeping her voice calm and low. "Yosef, Fanya has changed. She isn't the same young woman you met more than ten years ago. You've been here enough through the past year to have seen the change in her."

"Yes, of course, and I am not the same man I was when we first met," admits Yosef. "She was my total opposite. She had ardent revolutionary causes and I didn't know the difference between Bolsheviks and Mensheviks. I sought peace and balance and she was reckless and driven."

"How long were you together?" asks Fedora.

"Less than a year," says Yosef. "Then they took my Fanya to Siberia. I tried not to think about her but it was no use. Finally, I decided to find her."

The family stares at Fanya.

"Fanya, were you in Siberia for all that time?" asks Ivan.

"Yes."

"My dear," says Galayna, "That's at least nine years! We haven't heard of anyone surviving Siberia for that length of time. How were you able to survive?"

Fanya's nails pierce the skin on her hands. "Rage," she says.

"And do you still feel rage?" Galayna asks.

Fanya releases her fists, places her palm on her chest and studies the floor. "No," she says.

"Can you tell us how you got away?" Chingas asks.

Fanya looks up. "Explosives."

"Ah, yes. I heard about that," says Yosef. "Something about the dynamite for the railroad construction. It blew up an entire camp—killed everyone—even the guards. It shook the earth for a fifty-kilometer radius."

"Yes," says Fanya, smiling at Yosef.

"I'm so glad you were able to leave." Yosef lays his hand on Fanya's. "That is actually why I joined the Bolshevik Army. They let me work in intelligence, and I thought it would help me find my Fanya. Many of the people I worked with had known Fanya and they were also interested in finding her. I never stopped looking – not until I showed up here that day, and there she was."

"You worked in intelligence?" asks Chingas. "Wasn't that dangerous? They keep tabs on everything. Surely they knew you were trying to find a Siberian prisoner."

"In the revolutionary forces it was considered an honor to be sent to Siberia. Even Lenin was exiled. It's a matter of record. My work was never dangerous."

"Things have certainly changed in our government," says Chingas.

"What about now, Fanya?" Ivan asks. "Are you still interested in politics?"

Fanya turns her faded eyes toward Ivan. "No."

"So, Yosef, did you become a rebel as well?" asks Chingas.

A giggle erupts from Fanya. "Yosef, a rebel! I laugh at him in his uniform. He has no causes."

It is the first time Fanya has said more than a simple sentence, and the family exchanges delighted glances.

Yosef takes her hand and moves to look into her "Fanya, I know this may be sudden, but I must ask. I am b sent to Moscow in two days. I want you to come with me. I'll gone all winter, and I cannot bear to be apart from you."

Fanya's expression changes to pain. She removes her hand from Yosef's and wraps her arms around her legs, lowering her head to her knees. Yosef reddens, clenches his jaw and pushes his back against the wall. No one dares breathe, until…

"Aha," booms Chingas. "What do you think about a new chicken coop, Ivan – are Igor and Sol strong enough to help cut some sticks?"

Ivan lamely nods at his father. Everyone waits.

Fedora stands. "Please excuse me. I must tuck the children in."

"I can help you," says Galayna. Fanya follows the two women out the door.

The men linger a short time before walking Yosef to his wagon.

# CHAPTER 6
## *May 1917-1918*

The Meinrel's bountiful harvest of 1917 fills their larder. Fedora only allows Fanya and Dagmar at her family dinner table, instructing the other guests to forage for food in the woods. Before the trees lose their leaves, Franco and the others venture off to find their way back to places they lived prior to their imprisonment. After the first frost, Fanya and the Meinrel children move into the cozy barn with Dagmar and her baby.

November and December are warmer than usual, but a long and bitter cold snap accompanies January 1918, keeping the family huddled around embers. Now it is the middle of February 1918, and a rare storm keeps the family hunkered inside for a week. The wind picks up, blowing snow in circles and making warmth impossible. Late one night Fedora climbs the ladder to the sleeping loft she shares with her husband. She has been helping Dagmar with her sick baby.

"Are the children all right?" Ivan asks.

"They are all right. Dagmar's baby has died. Dagmar actually seems relieved. It's been such a difficult struggle for that little one. It's too cold for a burial."

"I'll try to find enough wood to build something to protect her body in the snow until the earth thaws."

"I think Dagmar was expecting this. She has some large rocks in the corner of the barn to cover the body. Poor Fanya is inconsolable. I believe she lost her own child, and she is taking this extremely hard."

"If that's the case perhaps she can finally face her demons. She has come a long way over the past few months."

"I hope you're right," says Fedora, snuggling next to him. Exhaustion sets in quickly and she snores softly before Ivan returns to sleep.

Early the next morning, Fedora and Galayna prepare a small meal to take to the barn. They hold the gruel close and brace themselves against the cold. The wind blows even stronger this morning, and they hang onto one another, planting each step in the drifts until they're inside the barn.

"Mama," Chana says tearfully. "Fanya is gone. She wasn't here when I awoke. Where could she have gone on such a night?"

Fedora gives gruel to Chana. "The snow would have covered her tracks. Maybe she went to talk with Rabbi Wecht, Chana. She was very mournful about the baby's death. We must help Dagmar now."


IN THE SPRING of 1918, Yosef brings a loaded wagon drawn by his old mare.

"Yosef! Yosef!" Otto shouts. The six-year-old bounds down the hill, almost tackling Yosef.

"My goodness, Otto! You are at least a hand taller, and your hair is redder. I think you have been eating too many carrots," Yosef teases.

"Yup. Too many carrots."

Yosef laughs and the rest of the family joins them.

"Oh, my," exclaims Yosef when he sees Chana, sixteen, and Amalie, fifteen. "I thought it was impossible for the two of you to get more beautiful, but here you are, grown and enchanting." Chana and Amalie smile.

Yosef looks past the gathering. Ivan breaks the news. "I hate to tell you this, Yosef, but Fanya left nearly three months ago. She didn't tell us she was going. Please, my friend, come inside."

Yosef grabs the edge of the wagon and turns away from his greeters. "Why? Why, Fanya? Why would you go?"

"We were hoping she would return, but we have no idea where she went. She was upset when Dagmar lost her baby," Ivan says.

"Help me unload these commodities," orders Yosef, wiping his face on his sleeve. "They were discarded in Moscow and I thought you might have some use."

"Discarded, indeed!" exclaims Galayna. "These foodstuffs are fresh. Yosef, there is no way to thank you for saving our family so many times. Chingas has regained his healthy, thanks to you. I wish we could give something back."

"You did," says Yosef. "Let's go to the house. I must know all about my Fanya."

The family sorrowfully relates the circumstances about Fanya, and how she left unexpectedly the night of the great storm. Yosef looks stricken. He joins them for dinner, but eats little. After dinner he sleeps in his wagon, and in the morning he invites Chingas to go for a ride. At the train station he hands the reins to Chingas.

"Chingas, my friend. This is now your old mare and wagon. I will not be needing it in Moscow."

"Yosef, it is too much."

"No, my friend. I cannot repay your family for all you have done for Fanya, as well as others who suffered under the tsar. I know all your refugees are now gone, even my Fanya, but this is a gift from the party for all you have done. You cannot refuse."

"The party, ha! They only take! Oh, I'm sorry, Yosef. I don't know why I said that. I thank you, and the party, for this overly-generous gift." He places a fatherly hand on Yosef's shoulder. "Look, my young friend, I will inquire again about Fanya. Perhaps she made it to a neighboring community."

"She could not have survived that storm. I don't understand her. I thought we could finally be peaceful together."

"Yosef, she survived Siberia. I'm sure she is alive. Perhaps you cannot see it, but Fanya has a restlessness even when she is quiet. It might be what you love about her. Don't wish it away too quickly."

Yosef takes a large breath and nods. "My friend, if I ever find her again, I'm not sure what I will do."

The two shake hands, and Chingas waves as he proudly commands his new mare forward.

In Moscow Yosef pours himself into his work, choking back thoughts of Fanya, and receives awards and advancement in the Bolshevik's new military regime.


IN MID-SUMMER, 1918, Yosef again returns to the Meinrels, hoping for word of Fanya but discovers she has not been heard from the previous year. He gives them gifts from Moscow, for which the family expresses gratitude. The Meinrel children coax him into staying the night, and the women make extra preparations for a feast, celebrating the return of their friend and benefactor.

Otto commandeers Yosef into boosting him up a tree he determines to climb, and Yosef watches in alarm as the little boy missiles upward until the tree bends.

"Otto, Otto, come down. Please, Otto. Please be careful," Yosef calls time and again.

Otto allows his weight to bend the uppermost branch until he is hanging by one arm. With his free arm he catches hold of a neighboring treetop, then three more and back again.

"Yosef is getting a glimpse of our monkey," comments Ivan, setting down the tiny vegetables he has thinned from the garden.

"That he is," agrees Fedora. "I have decided it's better not to watch Otto when he climbs."

"He doesn't understand his own mortality," grumbles Galayna.

Around the dinner table, Yosef describes Otto's slithering up the tree and riding treetops in circles above him, and the family laughs.

"And when he comes down," Yosef continues, "It's literally jumping from branch to branch. Otto, you have no fear! We need you in the ranks, my boy. You could show a thing or two to the troops!"

"Yes, I could," says Otto, grinning.

The family chuckles and Yosef pinches his youngest friend on the cheek. Yosef looks up, smiling towards Fanya's empty seat, and then looks sick. He doesn't finish his meal.

When it's time for bed, Otto coaxes his family to let him sleep in the wagon with his best friend, Yosef, but the family declines, letting Yosef decide.

"Not tonight, Otto," replies Yosef to the begging youth. He turns to Chingas. "I need to finish my mourning and be done with it. I cannot take these ghosts with me when I leave tomorrow. It has stolen years of my life. I must untether my soul from Fanya. Tonight I must be alone."

Otto stops coaxing and each member of the family embraces Yosef and bids him sweet dreams. Early the next morning Chingas drives Yosef to the train station.

"Chingas, you know Fanya was right. The tsar and his family were executed," says Yosef.

"The children?"

"All shot."

"No!"

"Yes. They wanted to go to England but King George withdrew the invitation and someone, or a group of some sort, cornered them in their highway house and killed them."

"Are you sure it wasn't Lenin and the Bolsheviks?"

"I'm sure. I'm a Bolshevik and I'd never shoot them. No one knows for sure who did it."

"That is sad. There is one good thing—they loved each other. You know, Yosef, I've been thinking of what you said—about untethering your soul from Fanya."

"Aye, Chingas. I must. I feel like a prisoner, bound by something I can't even see."

"I know a lot about being tethered—the fears of being constantly targeted by strangers—watching loved ones starve, being raided and shot just for sport. That's what I call being tethered."

"Yes, my friend. You know more than anyone else about that. Yet you are optimistic and strong. How do you do it?"

"I found a way to be free. I know I can be killed, but they can never stop me from loving. Loving is a gift—a feeling of complete freedom. If you wish to be untethered, don't choose to be untethered from love."

"Loving Fanya robs me of peace—of life. What if she is suffering?"

"Fanya survived Siberia and then escaped from it, and I suspect she took out a whole camp in the process. She's my hero, Yosef. I could see that Siberia haunted her, but I would bet she survived that winter storm. She's quite a woman, Yosef—well worth your love."

"Perhaps. But a soldier must be strong. My comrades tell me that all this worry is making me weak. They tell me I have to let her go."

"I hope you find peace, Yosef."

"Chingas, is that the same old mare I gave you?"

"It is."

"Why would I give you such an old mare? I need to bring you a new one."

"No. I like this one. We go the same speed."

"Aye, Chingas, my friend. I understand. Thank you for the ride."


A MONTH AFTER Yosef returns to Moscow, he receives advancement in his security office, achieving the rank of chief, overseeing military and government provisions. If memories of Fanya Kaplan creep into his mind, he shuts them out quickly, and buries himself in military discipline.

On August 30, 1918, Lenin speaks to two thousand workers at a Moscow factory. At the end of the speech, which sounds like all the others to Yosef, Yosef returns to his office, but is soon interrupted by a courier.

"Commander, sir," reports the young cadet. "There has been a shooting – an assassination attempt on Vladimir Lenin."

"What! I was just there. The Vladimir was fine!"

"It was when he was leaving sir, just before he stepped into his vehicle. He was shot thrice."

"Shot three times? Is he dead?"

"No, he lives."

"Who would do such a treasonous act!" Yosef demands.

"The traitor was caught and arrested on the spot, sir, and will be shot tomorrow at first light. The security director has given you the honor of commanding the firing squad."

"Me? But I only oversee provisions. I didn't know the director was even aware of me. This is unexpected." Yosef stands straighter.

"The director knows everything about everyone."

"The police usually take care of discipline," Yosef says.

"Not with a national traitor of this level. It must be assigned to an officer. You have been appointed."

"Please tell the director I am honored to be chosen. I shall do my best. Where is this traitor?"

"She is in the lower dungeon of the citadel at Red Square."

"She?" asks Yosef, paling.

"Yes. A blond woman. Very pretty. She actually met with the Vladimir prior to the speech."

Yosef turns his back and dismisses the cadet. He sits in a chair and places his head between his knees. "Please, God. Please don't let it be Fanya."

# CHAPTER 7
## *September 1918*

Fanya fights for consciousness, focusing on the voices on the other side of the thick cell door.

"Yosef," she whispers, "You have found me." Odors of human excrements fill her nostrils, and she considers the embarrassing filth of her presentment. In the darkness of her prison, she wiggles her small body across the gritty floor until she reaches the wall and forces her broken back to a sitting position, using the cold concrete wall as support. She wishes she could brush back her wild blond hair, or wipe the blood from her face, but her arms no longer respond. A large lock of hair covers her eyes, and she blows hard to move it aside, but the weighty tress sticks. She sees movement through the cracks in the massive wood door, and hears keys jangle in the lock. As he enters, the light is behind him, silhouetting his uniform, and even now his presence excites her. The guard leaves the door ajar to allow light, and she watches Yosef's rigid stance, waiting until they are alone and his eyes have adjusted to the darkness.

She feels joyous relief and peace. Now she can finally share Zoë with him. He will be comforted to know that his lover and his daughter will be together — that neither will be alone.

As the last sounds of the guard's receding footsteps disappear beyond the cell door, Fanya watches Yosef's frame relax, and he stoops down to look into her eyes. She knows he has not slept, and she reads the pain and confusion she has caused this gentle man yet again. How can she explain so he will understand?

She remembers the night her anger returned—the night Dagmar's baby died. Another baby lost to starvation! She confronted the ugly aftermath of the utopian ideals she had fostered in the revolution. People – entire villages – dead and dying in greater numbers than they had under tsarism. She could see Lenin usurping the power that rightfully belonged to the people. The horrible storm of that night was no match for the storm inside Fanya's soul. After months of dormancy the fire inside her ignited and burned more fervently than ever. She headed for Moscow, gathering a few of her revolutionary comrades en route.

After months of heated debate Lenin finally acquiesced to right the wrongs in a public address in Moscow. Fanya had encouraged people into the square. She was shocked when Lenin rebuked the ideals she held so dear. He had the gall to proclaim himself ruler. His speech attacked the freedoms she cherished, and for which even little Zoë had died. When Lenin's ninety-minute speech ended, a few people cheered, but her comrades shouted angry questions, which Lenin ignored.

As the self-proclaimed Vladimir made his way to his waiting automobile, Fanya found herself directly in front of him. She does not recall taking the small gun from her pocket – was it just yesterday? She heard the pistol fire three times, and watched Lenin's expression turn from horror to shock before he fell. She was immediately arrested, and it had been a blur of torture and pain since then.

"Yosef. I knew you would come."

Their eyes cannot break the gaze. "Fanya, my poor Fanya. I cannot save you. I cannot save you," he cries. "You shot the Vladimir of the revolution—your revolution, Fanya. Why? Why? Don't tell me. It doesn't matter." He sobs.

"Yosef, sweet Yosef," she whispers. "I could not come to you. I wanted to but you were so…so very serious about your soldiering." She smiles. "I couldn't compromise you. I had to try to fix it on my own."

"Fanya," he finally blurts. "I have drawn the duty of overseeing your firing squad."

"Oh, my darling – I am sorry. This will be difficult for you."

Yosef lowers his head to Fanya's lap to muffle the sounds, and she winces as his head touches her legs. Fanya closes her eyes. "Think!" she commands herself.

"Yosef, it isn't coincidence that you were picked for this duty. Someone—an enemy, or even a friend, is using our relationship in this political nightmare." She tries to kick him with her knee but it doesn't obey. "Yosef, you must listen, please Yosef. You have no mind for politics, but they know of us. They know of everyone. Yosef, listen to me, please! You have to help them." Fanya whispers and Yosef sobs.

"Yosef, there will be vying for position. Fingers will be flying to point the blame. What about the Meinrels?" She looks down at the suffering man crying in her lap and tries to kick him again. "You won't want to help me, but you must, Yosef. You must."

Yosef continues to sob, ignoring her.

"Yosef!" she yells. "There is no time for crying right now. Listen!" Yosef sits up like an obedient child.

"Yosef, you must go to Kovno and warn the Meinrel family. Their blood will be sought for vengeance. You must help them. Promise me, Yosef."

Yosef gazes at Fanya, disbelief in his eyes. "Have you learned nothing from—all this—this ugliness?" His words are hard and accusing.

"Yosef, if they know of us they will know of the Meinrel's. You have to warn them."

"Treason!" he shouts. He sniffs and gags at the smell. His facial expression is revulsion.

"Yosef, think of young Otto and those beautiful young women, Chana and Amalie. Yosef, you have to help them."

"I don't take my orders from a traitor. I take my orders from the Vladimir, and I am loyal. You know nothing of loyalty!" Yosef rises to his feet. "It would be a betrayal, Fanya – something I will never do. But you, Fanya, even in your final minutes, hideous as you are—your heart is still full of treason." He spits at her.

Fanya knows he will be able to give the order to the firing squad.

Yosef steps to the cell door and shouts orders. Almost immediately a small regiment enters the room. Two men lift Fanya from her crumpled position, ignoring her gasps of pain. They drag her up the stairs, and into the cool, bright morning. Each movement is torture, and she almost feels relief when they balance her against the cold execution wall. As the soldiers take their places with the squad, Fanya forces her posture as erect as she can and lifts her chin in defiance, facing the twenty men with loaded rifles. Generally a firing squad has two soldiers. She avoids looking at Yosef, but she hears his voice shout the orders, husky and wretched. It's better that he knows nothing of their daughter. At the remembrance of Zoë, calmness washes over Fanya, beginning at her breast and spreading outward, expanding through every cell. She can see Zoë twirling through myriads of vibrant flowers; beautiful Zoë, arms outstretched, running toward her. The vision delights Fanya, and she smiles as bullets fly toward her body.

# CHAPTER 8
## *January 1919*

January 2, 1919, Yosef jumps from the train at the station nearest Kovno. At this late hour the village sleeps. He looks toward the horse-masters, and decides to walk the three kilometers to Rabbi Wecht's home.

The winter night is clear, and Yosef ignores the dancing aurora as his boots squeak over the snow. He cares little that his face and limbs are growing numb, yearning for the moment that his heart becomes numb as well.

A few minutes later he approaches the rabbi's comfortable dwelling near the edge of Kovno. The empty lot in front shows almost no trace of the synagogue ruins. Yosef circles the house to the back stoop and bangs firmly on the door, bangs again, and again.

"Coming; I'm coming," he hears the rabbi calling. He sees the light of a lantern, and hears the shuffling of footsteps. The door opens, revealing Rabbi Wecht in his nightdress. The rabbi balances eyeglasses on his nose and holds up a lantern, gazing into the darkness to identify the late caller.

"Yosef! I was praying you would come, so this is my fault I suppose. Next time I'll pray for a day-time visit. Ah, well, come in, come in, my son." Yosef follows the rabbi and his lantern into the main room where the host motions toward a settee. Yosef sits and the rabbi pulls a stool in front of Yosef and plunks down. He places the lantern on the floor, lighting the two men's facial features from beneath, and throwing shadows across their faces.

"Sorry, Rabbi, but this could not wait until tomorrow. I am here to fulfill Fanya's last request."

The old rabbi studies his guest.

"Yosef. How is your marriage to – Katrina? Is that her name?"

"Yes, Rabbi. Katrina is fine. How did you find out?"

"You have your sources, I have mine. Let's see, you have been married almost four months, Yosef, and most of that time you have been away from your new bride. It is nice that you can finally come home. So, have you been home to see Katrina, or did you come directly here?"

"No, I did not go home. I came straight here from the station."

"Aha," says the rabbi. "Yosef, I must say this. It is my calling, so give me latitude. Yosef, you married Katrina too quickly after Fanya died – less than two months, I believe. Was that fair?"

"What do you mean, fair?"

"Katrina is young and beautiful and has a right to be loved by her husband. So, I ask you again? Was it fair? How could you have stopped loving Fanya, even if you willed yourself to?"

"But you remarried quickly after the death of your wife," Yosef says.

"Yes, but I can talk to my wife about Greta. You dare not breathe Fanya's name."

"Rabbi, please," Yosef moans. "I did not come here to discuss Fanya."

"No? And, you want me to hear her last request? How can you not talk of her?" The rabbi moves closer to Yosef and places his hand on Yosef's shoulder. "I know you feel unspeakable

63

pain." The rabbi draws in air through his nostrils. "I smell your agony."

Yosef buries his face in his hands and his shoulders shake. "Rabbi, how can you know this? I have told no one."

"It is my curse to know these things."

"Did you know I was there when Fanya was shot?"

"No. I didn't know that. Oh, my boy, how tragic."

"Did you know I was the one who ordered the firing squad?"

Rabbi Wecht gasps. "Oh no, Yosef. I did not know. I am so so sorry, my son."

Yosef clenches his fists, hunches down, and beats on the sides of his head. "I hear my voice say, 'fire' and I hear the guns!" He lays his head on his knees. "Why did I tell them to fire?" Yosef sits up and speaks, his voice is high-pitched and overly slow.

"You should have seen her, Rabbi." Yosef wipes his face on his sleeve. "Oh my, she was glorious. She faced twenty gunmen, so small against the backdrop of the Red Square, daring them. Just before she died, the most joyful smile crossed her face. I thought she might laugh but the bullets got there too fast. I cannot forget it, Rabbi. I cannot forget anything about her – what she said, how she moved, her expressions – it's like they're all inside of me, and every day they grow larger no matter how I fight against them."

"Especially when you can't talk with anyone about her," says the rabbi. "I have felt your pain."

Yosef bites his quivering lips. "When I awake next to Katrina and see black hair instead of blond spread across the pillow, my pain begins. When Katrina kisses me and I open my eyes, I revile because it isn't Fanya. You're right, Rabbi. It is not fair." Yosef's sleeve continues to mop as water streams from his eyes and nose. "You know what they call her, Rabbi? What they call my Fanya? Death woman."

The rabbi gulps loudly and repeats the phrase in a whisper. "Death woman! Toppur knew it." The rabbi shakes his head.

"It hurts to hear them talk about her," Yosef says.

"Why did you come here in the coldness, when everyone is asleep? What is it you want me to do, Yosef?"

Yosef smears his face against his sleeve and lets his lungs collapse as his eyes take on a distant stare. This statement will fulfill his final purpose. His facial muscles relax and he listens to the silence. He draws in air and delivers his message. "Fanya said the Meinrels are in danger. Lenin will seek vengeance when he discovers that they helped her. You must warn them."

"But, Yosef. Why should I warn them?"

Yosef frowns. "I didn't expect to negotiate with you, Rabbi. This is Fanya's final request, and you are the Meinrel's friend. Surely you will honor her wish that they be warned."

"You and Fanya spent many a night breaking bread with that family. Do you not consider each one, from Chingas the patriarch to young Otto, a friend?"

"Of course I do, Rabbi, but I am a soldier."

"So?"

Yosef fidgets. "Rabbi, a soldier cannot go around warning villagers against soldiers. It is treason."

"Treason, Yosef? Is it treason for a good soldier to protect the people of his country? To protect his family? His friends? And, if you are right and it is treason, is it less treasonous to tell me instead of telling the Meinrels?"

Yosef breathes rapidly. "Of course, Rabbi, soldiers are supposed to protect the people," he explodes, pounding his knees with his fists, "but right now there is a lot of panic because of Fanya's attempt on the Vladimir's life. So instead of protecting people, soldiers must punish them."

"How would Fanya have felt about that?"

Yosef shakes his head. "That's the irony of it. What she has caused, she would hate."

"Are you sure she caused it, Yosef? Why are you so quick to blame Fanya? Perhaps Lenin caused it."

Yosef starts. "Such loose talk, Rabbi!"

"To me, Yosef, any talk against my loved ones is treason, and I loved Fanya." The rabbi softens. "I know you did too, more than all the rest of us combined. It must be grievous for you to hear her name slurred."

The pain in Yosef's gut intensifies. He clears his throat to get rid of the lump, but it grows as he speaks. "Yes, Rabbi. My soul dies more every single day since I killed her. I loved her from the moment I first saw her and my final thought will be of her."

"And you have decided that living without her is worse than death, am I right?"

"Yes. My pain is too great. I would welcome death rather than continue in this misery. I came to deliver Fanya's last request and then hope to die."

"Then, Yosef, my son, there is one way for you to make this count."

"I will do anything."

"Use your life, and your death, Yosef, to restore your honor. You must be a soldier for Fanya."

"How?"

The rabbi puts his face into Yosef's, almost touching noses. He raises his brows, opens his eyes wide and whispers. "There are only two questions for you to answer, young Yosef." The rabbi holds up one finger between their eyes. "First, can you live with this pain?"

"The answer is no, I cannot live with this pain," Yosef says.

He adds a second finger. "Second, will your death be wasted?"

The air between them stops, neither man breathing.

The rabbi draws away from Yosef and nods his head several times.

"Rabbi, I want to be a soldier for Fanya. I want to die for her. Please, please, tell me how to make my death count. Please help me rid myself of this wretchedness."

"If you do what I ask, Lenin will mark you a traitor."

"Like Fanya?"

"Yes, like Fanya," says the rabbi.

Yosef nods. "It would be all right if I am Fanya's soldier. I will die a traitor like her."

The rabbi nods. "Now, my son, how do you feel?"

Yosef stares at the rabbi. "My pain, it is better. It feels so much better. Yes, Rabbi, it feels right that I should be Fanya's soldier. I'll do whatever you tell me."

"Even treason?"

"Let them shoot me. It would be a relief. If I commit treason they will obliterate my name from history. It will be like I never existed."

"Like they did with Fanya?" asks Rabbi Wecht.

"Yes, like Fanya," Yosef whispers. His eyes don't blink when the fire pops. "Yes, Rabbi. Treason for Fanya. For me. For you. For my friends. Yes, I am Fanya's soldier now. I will do whatever is needed to help my friends—like Fanya did."

The rabbi nods. "All right, Yosef, this is your first order. You must intercept information about targeted families and pass it to my contact in Moscow."

The lines in Yosef's face flatten out and his eyes sparkle. "I will, Rabbi. Can you see the change in me? I feel focused, confident and hopeful. I am willing, Rabbi, but I'm not sure I can help. Vladimir Lenin has been increasingly distant since Fanya's attempt. He is brutal and paranoid and he accuses everyone. He's given the Cheka a long arm to torture and punish. They enjoy terrorizing and they're very good at it. I'm not in a position to know their orders."

"Yosef, they're turning entire villages into mass graves. You must get the information. It won't be handed to you. You'll have to find a way to steal it. When you get it, pass it along or bring it here. If you die, you die. Do what you believe Fanya would do and I promise you will have peace."

Yosef swallows loudly. "I can feel the peace, Rabbi," he says, banging his fist on his chest. "I can feel Fanya and I know this is right. I will find a way, whatever happens. I was a walking dead man when I knocked on your door. Now I am alive. I have a purpose. I am Fanya's soldier. Thank you, thank you." Yosef kisses the rabbi fully on each cheek.

"Good. Then, in return, yes, I will go to the Meinrels and have a talk with them. You are right. They are in harm's way. Now come, Yosef. I have some quilts. You may use this floor."

"No, Rabbi. I must go to my house immediately. It is better that no one sees us together, especially since we are conspiring."

The two men rise and walk to the door.

Yosef gives a half grin. "I had no idea treason was so healing."

"And what of Katrina," questions the rabbi at the door. "She is innocent, you know, and will likely be a casualty. She can be a good wife, Yosef."

"You are right, Rabbi," Yosef admits. "I will try to be a better husband." He places his hat on his head and ducks into the night.

# CHAPTER 9
## *Fall 1920*

Yosef gropes the horse's head in the darkness. The bony old mare resists his clumsy hands as he claws around her nose, pinching her lips with the bridle. She snorts objections.

"I know you prefer the solitude of the barn to my awkward company but we have a mission—it will be our last and most important," he whispers.

He latches the bridle slightly askew, and she shakes her head to adjust the comfort.

"It's all right, come on, one more time. Most of the leaves have fallen, so you'll have a soft cushion to walk on."

Shadows from the house outline Katrina's face pressed against the window—his energetic thoughtful young wife who doesn't seem to notice that he only feels a passing pleasure for her.

Katrina, the ideal soldier's wife, happily entertains herself during his long absences and only mildly objects when he departs. Whenever Yosef returns, her loveliness surprises him. But Fanya's ghost makes it impossible to enjoy marriage with Katrina. Moments after returning home from assignments, restlessness overwhelms him and he rushes away, feigning excuses, like he did at three this morning.

Katrina is the political-opposite of Fanya. His wife entirely missed the torrents of the revolution, which were so much a part of Yosef's and Fanya's youth. Katrina enjoys baking from her ample pantry, untouched by the deprivations of the Russian population. Katrina never questions authority, and carefully complies with regulations—dutiful, predictable Katrina. She told him of her plans for a dinner party to celebrate their second anniversary, but he doubts he'll be alive for it.

Yosef thinks about his many treasonous acts over the past eighteen months. He feels important to Rabbi Wecht's organization, The People's Protectors. The ongoing demands of intrigue excite Yosef and give him hope for atonement with Fanya. He often goes to villages personally to warn of impending annihilation. It frustrates him when people ignore his high-risk warning, telling themselves there is no reason for anyone to kill them, as if the soldiers care about who they murder.

Just last week Yosef saw the names of the Meinrel family on an advice memorandum, which he hastily destroyed. But last evening he discovered the orders of the Cheka to annihilate Kovno and he caught the midnight train home. Yosef will warn Kovno, particularly the Meinrel family and Rabbi Wecht, that the Cheka will attack and annihilate their village today.

Katrina, peering through the window, her black heavy braid draped over her shoulder, stark against her white nightdress, apologized for harping at him about not wearing his uniform. She had said, "I hope my parents are wrong about you." He wonders how much her parents know.

At the edge of the woods Yosef tightens the saddle and hefts himself over the mare's back patting her to move forward. He repositions the gun in his holster and digs his heels into the soft flanks. Thoughts of Katrina evaporate.

Yosef relishes moments like this where he can be alone with run-away lamentations for Fanya. Even after two years, regret and grief fill his soul and he wallows in misery at every opportunity. Alone in the darkness, he immerses himself in his obsession. Plodding along he raises his dark eyes toward the heavens. The crisp air and sparkling stars mark tracings of a fast-approaching winter. He watches the tailing of a star falling from the sky.

"Fanya, Fanya. Forgive me, my love," he begs. "Let me feel you near to me, my darling. I am so sorry." Tears well up in his eyes, blurring the celestial brilliance. The back of his neck relaxes, allowing his heavy head to bob against the top of his spine. A familiar lump fills his throat and the muscles in his face twist in pain, all the while moving forward rhythmically on the back of his mare.

Fifty minutes from the time he left his house Yosef enters the sleeping Jewish colony of Kovno. He dries his eyes and breathes deep. He guides his mare past the windmill to the rabbi's home, and bangs on the front door. Within seconds the door creeks open.

"Yosef, don't you ever sleep?"

"Rabbi, the Cheka will be upon Kovno at first light. Come quickly. We must warn the people."

Rabbi Wecht's facial expression drops in horror. He shakes his head and grabs his coat and boots, putting them on as he moves out the door.

"Do you think they will save themselves?" asks Yosef.

"That is not our concern. Some may be responsive. It is up to us to warn, Yosef. What they do with it is up to them."

"Many just sit and talk themselves out of believing, Rabbi," says Yosef. "I have risked my life to warn people who do nothing. Nothing!"

"A common complaint among religious leaders, Yosef."

"I'm serious, Rabbi. The early warning system seems wholly ineffective."

"Not wholly, Yosef. It warns. Come, my son. We must hurry. You run to the other end of town—tell the Meinrel family first. I'll begin at this end and enlist the help of some of the men. Then you must hurry back to your home or you will run right into the Cheka."

The rabbi stops and grabs Yosef's elbow. "I appreciate your warning, Yosef, but you know I cannot leave Kovno, right?"

"I know Rabbi," says Yosef.

The two men split up, and Yosef gallops his mare to the Meinrels. When he gets to the bend of the river, he tethers his mare to the grass and runs straight uphill and bangs on the front door.

Neighborly daytime calls are always at the back door. Front doors are for emergencies. Chingas opens the door wearing only his long handles and peers sleepily at Yosef, trying to focus.

"Yosef?"

Yosef watches the house enliven.

"I'm sorry to bring such bad news, but the Cheka will be upon Kovno at first light. You are in the path of destruction."

Galayna and Ivan join Chingas at the door.

"Yosef, thank you for coming," says Ivan. "Please come in."

"Ivan! You are all in imminent danger. You must hurry."

Chingas puts on his eyepatch and smiles at Yosef. "We knew it was you that sent the first warning almost eighteen months ago, even though the rabbi would not tell us."

"You are a blessing," says Galayna, kissing him.

Their pleasantries confuse Yosef but he snaps himself back to reality. "This is not a social call."

Ivan speaks for the family. "Yosef, thank you for your warning. Mother has been praying for months that we would get even an hour of final warning before the Cheka's descent upon our village. You are an answer to her prayers."

"Aye," agrees Chingas.

Yosef blows air through his lips. "My friends, I must hurry to your neighbors to spread the word. I wish you well," and with that Yosef bounds back to his mare. The Meinrels wave at their friend and close the door.


Ivan and Fedora run to the barn to awaken the children.

"Chana, Amalie. Arise quickly. You must get ready to leave, just as we planned," urges Fedora. "We have a risk to take today."

"Mother! Now? Right now?" Chana sobs as she awakens. "We have to go away and leave you now?"

"Yes, my daughter. Now hurry. Your father is waking Otto, and he's only eight, so you mustn't let him see your dread," Fedora scolds.

Amalie sits up. "Chana, everything will be all right," she says. "We just have to keep saying what we always say: 'It is a risk, but a worthy risk that must be taken.'"

"It is a risk, but a worthy risk that must be taken," recites Chana, fighting tears.

"How did Otto take the news?" Fedora asks Ivan as they pack precious commodities into barrels.

"He's excited. He believes we will be joining them in Germany."

"That is best, I think," says Fedora.


Down the road Yosef bangs on the last door. After leaving the occupants full of fear and trepidity, he decides to walk his frothing mare. Retracing his steps, he sees lanterns burning through the window of a cabin where adults huddle together talking excitedly.

"Fools," he chides bitterly to his mare. "You are probably telling one another that the Cheka have no reason to harm your family." He kicks a rock. "Your children will die; you will die; why don't you flee?"

The nostrils of his horse snort, sending cloudy puffs into the cool darkness of the morning. Yosef guides his horse to the Meinrel's. He sees some movement outside their small dwelling. Old Chingas leads the mare Yosef gave him three years before, hitching it to the flatbed wagon. Chingas's mare is much older than Yosef's. Yosef stops to assist his old friend.

"Thank you, Yosef. We were just saying the other day that we wish you would stop by. And now you have, bringing us the warning we have prayed would come. I have silently hoped it would be you that brought it," pants the old man.

"So, you're leaving?" Yosef asks.

"I am, with the children."

"And what of Fedora, and Ivan, and Galayna? They will not be spared!"

"We have to hope, Yosef, because the Cheka cannot learn that the children have left. Ivan, Fedora and Galayna will stay to assure we aren't tracked. Besides, we barely have enough rations to get the children to Germany. Since your first warning, we have been on half rations, setting aside all we could for this trek. It is good that we were able to get some of the harvest in. Once I get the children safely to Germany I will sell this horse and wagon to get passage for them to a safer place. Galayna, Ivan and Fedora will join us when they can."

Yosef watches the twitch in the corner of his friend's good eye, and realizes the heartbreak of the decision. Yosef wants to object, but he has brought nothing to offer the family, and he regrets that he had not aided their predicament sooner.

"Chingas – at least take my mare. She is old, but not as old as this one."

"No thank you, Yosef. You have done aplenty, and this old mare and I, we understand each other. She will do what is required."

Grandmother Galayna, in her black work dress, rolls a large barrel toward the wagon. Her thick gray braids, usually twisted in rings, swing free, knocking her shawl from her shoulders.

"Yosef, you're back" she greets with a kiss and embraces him, not releasing her clasp. "What you do is good, Yosef. You see our barrels. They are full of provisions for the children. It will help Chingas get them to safety. If you had not warned us, we would not be able to save them."

As Yosef helps her with the barrel he aches to scream "But what about you, Galayna? What about Ivan and Fedora?" But he holds his silence, accepting and hating their decision. At his home, Katrina's pantry could sustain this entire family for a trip to Germany, but that will not help them now, and the familiar acid of disdain expands in his chest and stomach. Would Fanya have helped them more?

Chingas climbs onto the wagon and Yosef hoists up the first barrel.

Galayna answers Yosef's silent question. "It is enough, Yosef. After doing all we can, we commend our safety, and the safety of our children, into God's hands. He makes miracles of such things. All is well here, Yosef."

Yosef cannot argue with such wishful logic. He has seen the aftermath of the Cheka, and Galayna's God is no match. Galayna rushes to the house while Yosef rolls the other barrel into position and heaves the barrel toward his old friend. Chingas grabs for it, pulling it sideways onto the flatbed. Yosef breathes hard, re-playing Galayna's last words over again in his mind. How can Galayna's miraculous God help children who will be crossing three—maybe four countries in the hardest part of winter? His anger surfaces.

"Chingas," he explodes, "How in blazes will you find your way to Germany – provided you actually make it past the forest marauders with three children?"

"It's my job, Yosef. We are of German descent and speak the language. I've crossed the borders into Poland and Germany twice before. I've been close to Bremen and, God willing, the children will be safely aboard a freedom ship in three months."

Yosef feels a little relief knowing that old Chingas has experience on the roadway, and heaves against the last barrel.

Chingas ropes the barrels in place. Galayna returns with an armload of clothing for her husband. Chingas steps from the flatbed and takes the bundle from her and dons the simple garb on top of his ragged sweaters. The patch over his left eye shifts as he hastily slips a poncho over his head, and his wife straightens the patch as well as the poncho. He places his battered top hat on his balding head and Galayna pats his chest to pronounce him ready. As she starts to turn away he grabs her elbow and their eyes hold until tears roll.

Chingas helps Galayna climb onto the wagon bed. She removes the lids of each barrel, inspecting the contents then replaces the lids with a firm pounding. Chingas watches her and Yosef notices that Chingas's chin quivers.

"My friend," Yosef says, extending his hand. "This is a time for your family. I will see if I can help Rabbi Wecht. I wish you well."

Chingas embraces and kisses Yosef.


Inside the Meinrel house candles flicker as Ivan and the three children move blankets and provisions. Fedora dresses in a corner. Her hands shake as she buttons up her Sabbath dress and brushes her auburn hair into a rush of curls, pinning them on top of her head.

"Don't let them see your dread," she whispers to herself. "They will remember you like this, so let them have a good memory." She opens the bureau and retrieves a small box, opens it and picks up the broach. She takes a second to gaze at it. She hears Ivan behind her and goes to him. He pulls her close and hugs her tight.

"It's okay, Fedora," he says.

She steps back and looks at him.

"Thank you for your calmness," she says. She takes a deep breath, straightens her posture and pins the broach to her dress.

Ivan steps to the door and calls Otto, who runs in from the barn. Otto hasn't bothered to comb his unruly hair and Fedora decides not to chase him with her comb today. He will wear his hat. Ivan puts his arm around Otto and leads him outside to help place provisions into the wagon. With the task completed they move the rig to the roadway in front of the house.

Fedora finds her two daughters on the back porch. She brings them silently into her arms and kisses them. Before they can cry, she helps them on with their long, fur-trimmed coats, and fusses with placing their hats over their black curls, avoiding their large, somber eyes. Fedora removes the broach from her breast.

"Amalie, you are seventeen and I want you to have this broach which belonged to my mother." Amalie closes delicate white fingers around the broach and holds it to her heart. Fedora removes the ring from her right hand.

"Chana, at eighteen you are a woman. I want you to have my ring." She places it on Chana's slender finger. Her daughters would linger, but Fedora takes their hands and moves them towards the rest of the family gathered at the road. She stands them firmly together behind the waiting wagon, and touches each of their faces.

Fedora turns to Otto. She wants to lose herself in his deep blue eyes, but cannot risk letting him glimpse her heartbreak. She inspects his clothing and tucks his muffler into the collar of his jacket.

"Is Amalie crying?" asks Otto.

Fedora glances at her daughters, unbidden tears dropping hot against their crimson cheeks. Without changing posture or expression, each girl flicks her cheeks as if there were annoying insects.

"Of course not," Fedora says. "Amalie just wants to get started."

Fedora walks to Chingas. "Your leg should hold. Keep it wrapped like I showed you if it feels weak."

"Aye," says Chingas looking at the stars. "It will hold. Thank you, daughter." He kisses her forehead.

Chingas approaches Ivan. "This winter will be a harsh one, but we are blessed to have the harvest." He kisses his son on each cheek and Ivan returns the kisses.

The family stands quietly for a moment studying one another, their breath clouding the morning air.

"Chingas, Ivan," says Galayna. "I must hear the Shema. Please. No one can stop us today."

The family quiets. The tsars outlawed Hebrew prayers years before, and the village elders complied. With Lenin's paranoia and social reforms, anti-Semitic punishments increased, so the men haven't sung the Shema for years.

Ivan and Chingas step together and begin the prayer shakily.

"Hear, Israel, the Lord is our God, the Lord is One." The two men hold on to one another, feeling for the old familiar cadence. Their voices blend richly as they increase the depth and tempo. "Blessed be the Name of His glorious kingdom for ever and ever; And you shall love the Lord your God with all your heart and with all your soul and with all your might..." The men increase volume and vigor. When they finish, they stand mutely facing one another. Chingas and Ivan nod, and Ivan steps toward his mother.

"Thank you," breathes Galayna, eyes glistening.

Chingas turns his attentions to the mare's attachments. When he completes his tasks at the wagon, he stands between his two granddaughters, who are still flipping away hot tears. Amalie steps closer to her grandfather and takes his arm. He flexes his bicep muscle.

Fedora pulls a handkerchief from her sleeve and wipes Otto's nose. She looks at his face and pulls him close.

"Mama?" he says.

She turns him quickly to face his father. Ivan gazes into the boyish face and sees tears surfacing. He tosses Otto's curly red hair and Otto tries to smile. Ivan firmly places Otto's hat on his head and shakes it. Otto grins.

"Take care of your sisters," Ivan instructs, steering his young son's footsteps toward his two older sisters and grandfather.

Otto pulls the fur hat from his head and enthusiastically waves it at his mother, father and grandmother, who are only a few feet away. Fedora smiles at her little boy, so full of spirit. Galayna walks to Otto and replaces his hat. Otto runs to the front of the wagon and tugs on the old mare's reigns, but the mare remains staid. "Come on! We're going to Bremen!" he shouts. The horse reluctantly digs her hooves into the hard ground seeking leverage to budge the loaded wagon.

"Look! I made the wagon move!" he yells.

Fedora leans against Ivan, watching her children. Galayna walks to her granddaughters and kisses them, and gives her husband a nod. Chingas turns away, training his eyes to the road. Galayna walks over to take her place beside Ivan, whispering her chant, "faith, faith, faith."

Chingas takes the reins from Otto. The horse obeys the soft clicking of his tongue, and the wagon creaks and jerks over the clumps of grass to the path that will take them northward. Chana and Amalie trail the lumbering wagon with heavy footsteps.

Fedora, Ivan and Galayna remain staid until the wagon is out of sight.

"We must be quick," says Fedora, running to the house.

"We need to erase all evidence of the children," says Ivan. "With luck, the day's bedlam will divert attention away from them."

"I'll check the barn," says Galayna.

"Put on your warmest clothing," Fedora says. "Tuck socks into your pockets."

Ivan walks to her and brings her into his arms. "It's all right, Fedora. Everything is all right. Our children will live. I feel peace."

She buries her face against him and cries.


At the other end of town, Yosef Roseman talks softly to his mare. "Your barn is waiting for you. See the daylight coming? Step lively or we'll surely meet the Cheka." Yosef continues to move through the woods, far enough off the main road. The lathering old mare slows so he dismounts and walks her.

Katrina will be waiting in their warm bed, and will make him welcome. If he can make it home he will be safe.

"Fanya, Fanya, can you hear me? I have kept your last request. The Meinrel children will be saved. Old Chingas is taking them to Bremen, Germany." A stick snaps under his boot and he jumps.

Suddenly Fanya's intense eyes blaze holes through the darkness, and he withers in shame.

"I am sorry, I am sorry!" he cries. "Of course, you would have done more. You would have found a way to save all of them. So many women and children will be trudging to death camps. All the men, shot, Ivan and Rabbi Wecht among them. What can I do, Fanya? Please tell me what to do. You would have found a way to save Kovno. You would have done something much braver and more brilliant than I have done."

Yosef falls to his knees and the mare stops. "I cannot stand this pain one more day." He stiffens his posture and hardens his jaw. "I will never be a disappointment to you again, Fanya. I will save all of them, even if only for an extra minute."

Yosef guides his mare to the road and mounts. He kicks her flanks and the horse trots. He kicks again and again until she runs at a steady gallop. He bypasses the turnoff leading to his home. In the distance he hears the clanking of wagons and horses of the Cheka. Yosef slides his pistol from the holster and cocks it firmly.

"Yes, Fanya. I feel it." He smiles.

# CHAPTER 10
## *Fall 1920*

The first day of their journey Chingas and the children walked in such a pall they didn't notice the weather. Yesterday it drizzled most of the day. This morning everything smells fresh and sun rays stream through the treetops. Amalie walks beside the mare, holding the bridle. Chingas hobbles alongside the wagon, hanging on to the flatboard to steady his gait, talking with Chana who walks beside him. Otto turns circles in the road ahead of Amalie, swatting the ground occasionally with a stick. He runs to a bridge and peers over the edge, drops his stick into the water and watches it float. Amalie stops, halts the horse, and leans her ear to the road ahead. Chana freezes and rests her hand on her grandfather's arm. Old Chingas runs to Amalie.

"Otto, come here, quick!" Amalie beckons to her little brother and he runs back to her. "Sh. Listen, Otto."

"It's dogs barking, and maybe some horses," Otto guesses.

Chingas's face pales. He keeps his voice low. "Quickly, children, off the road." He yanks the horse's reins to the right, leading her into a thicket. Amalie, Chana and Otto squat down in some brush, their eyes darting between their grandfather and the bridge at the curve in the roadway. The sounds are unmistakable: dogs barking, sounds of wagons rolling, horses snorting, and noises from men—many men—approaching rapidly.

The thicket in front of Chingas is congested and thorny but the old man ignores the thrashing against his face and hands and continues to push and pull the horse into the brush. The mare balks as thorns scrape her skin, but Chingas wrestles her forward until branches close behind the back of the wagon. Once in place, the horse quiets. Chingas fights his way out of the brambles and inspects the ground from the roadway. The cold earth left no marks. "Thank you, God," he utters. "Amalie, Chana, come quickly." Chingas lifts each granddaughter over the back of the wagon, avoiding the brambles, directing them to squirm over the front end of the flatbed until they are underneath the wagon and out of sight. "Lie down and don't come out, no matter what happens."

Except for Yosef, the family does not trust government soldiers. Peasant revolts are so common that Lenin granted his Red Army bullies the power to plunder or punish without accountability. Their insatiable appetites spare no one.

With his granddaughters secreted, Chingas scoops up Otto and runs back to the bridge. Otto giggles as he bounces under his grandfather's arm.

"I didn't know your broken leg could run," he laughs.

Chingas jumps off the edge of the bridge, and disappears underneath.

"Quiet, Otto," Chingas pants as he crams his grandson into a gap at the top of a stone pillar. Chingas moves to the opposite side of the bridge where he has a good vantage point of the thicket and crouches into the shadows. He doesn't hear his own heavy breathing as he ponders the deep barking noises. The large dogs are the most immediate threat to being discovered. Within minutes the tromping of horses, men and wagons over the wooden bridge are deafening. Cold sweat flows down Chingas's face, back, and underarms. The Red Army surrounds his grandchildren.

To his right Chingas tries to glimpse shadows, gauging the size of the troops lumbering overhead. The patch on his left eye prevents him from seeing the dog lapping water from the stream.

A wagon clears the bridge and Chingas hears the lapping. He stops breathing and slowly turns his head and sees the dog, a couple meters away. Another dog runs straight through the stream and past the lapping dog. The black dog runs after him, up the stream and away from Chingas, toward the thicket and his hidden granddaughters. The dogs turn playfully and run under the bridge, past Chingas and Otto, and dart up the bank, unaware of the paralyzed, sweating man in the shadows of the bridge. Chingas watches the dogs between him and the thicket. They play and run closer and closer to where Chana and Amalie are hiding.

Both dogs halt and look toward the thicket. One barks and runs toward it, and then the other joins him. Did the old mare make a sound? The dogs bark and dance and then they sniff the base of the thicket. One of them digs and growls and the other one joins him, digging under the thorns exactly where his granddaughters lay. Chingas is frozen with fear and whispers a prayerful plea. Chingas knows the dogs sense his terrified granddaughters. A sickness fills his stomach as he steps from the shadows and gives a shrill whistle.

The dogs' ears perk up in his direction. He places his fingers to his lips to whistle again but feels pressure from small hands shoving against his stomach. The unexpected shove catches him off-guard, and he falls backward into the stream, hidden in the shadows of the bridge.

"Stay here," Otto orders. "Papa told me to take care of my sisters." And with that, Otto runs out from under the bridge before Chingas can grab him, and quickly scales the embankment. The dogs snarl and growl when they see Otto, then charge the fur-covered lad, teeth showing. Otto freezes in place, eyes widening as the distance closes between him and the bloodthirsty animals.

Chingas sees his grandson stiffen. Chingas tries to jump to his feet, but his body reacts as if it is buried in sludge. The paralysis holds him prisoner as he watches the lead dog lunge at his grandson. A soldier's arm comes from nowhere and grabs the lad by the collar on his coat, and with the other he strikes the charging animal with a baton, sending him sailing and yelping. The second dog skids to a stop. Chingas clamors through his brain for something – anything – that will free his grandson from the hands of the lethal Red Army. His eyes dart around for some sort of bargaining chip, and he desperately searches his pockets. His eyes freeze on the bushes where the wagon is secreted. There are provisions in the wagon. Perhaps he can… Reason interrupts his runaway panic. He cannot use the wagon, or its contents. He cannot reveal that he has a wagon. He cannot even reveal his own existence for fear of leaving his granddaughters defenseless in this corrupt valley. His arms grab around his chest to keep his own heart from breaking as he realizes he has no power to influence the fate of his precious Otto. With his arms still clutched around him, he falls back into the shadows, his back hitting the side of moldy beams. Tears stream down his face, and sickness wells up in his stomach. He hears a soldier order the dogs tied to the back of a wagon, and then listens as his grandson is dragged to the edge of the bridge, just a few feet away. Chingas watches them through cracks in the rocks.

"What are you doing here?" demands the soldier.

Otto shrugs. "I'm going home. Where are you going?" The old man under the bridge almost smiles at the response.

"We'll ask the questions here," the soldier barks, and Chingas hears the wretched pop as the soldier's hand strikes Otto's cheek. Otto loses his balance and would have fallen if the soldier did not have hold of his coat. His hat tumbles from his head, down the embankment. Through hot tears, his grandfather watches it bounce on a rock and fall into the water. It floats to the edge of the wall whose shadows obscure a sorrowing presence.

Otto's head of bright red curls shines with sweat.

"Red hair!" exclaims the soldier. He releases Otto's coat. "I don't have time for children," he barks. "We'll get the truth out of you tonight." With that, the soldier throws Otto in the direction of two subordinates, who take charge of him, pushing him ahead of them as they rejoin the troop. Chingas reaches down and picks up the small furry hat and clutches it to his agonized breast.

# CHAPTER 11
## *Fall 1920*

Otto hears a muffled cry from the thicket as the soldier marches him past it, but he dares not glance in that direction. He stands straight and marches higher.

A few minutes later, plodding down the road, Otto stoops to pick up a stick and the soldier behind him knocks it away. After another hour of trudging, Otto runs to pick up a shiny rock.

"Get back in line," yells the soldier.

"But all we do is walk in a straight line," Otto says.

A soldier slaps his head. "Keep up, kid."

Otto ventures into conversation. "How come you just walk straight all the time? Don't you ever get to run or twirl or jump around?"

"Shut up, kid," warns the soldier, smacking Otto again. Otto falls down, and the soldier picks him up and throws him onto a wagon. "This kid's riding with you. He can't keep up."

"Yes, sir," replies the wagon driver.

Otto sits quietly beside the driver. The wagon just ahead of them is a flatbed, with two large, burly men riding on the back, sharpening long knives. Their heads are shorn, and dark hair covers their faces. One looks at Otto with hard, black eyes and Otto shivers and looks away.

The wagon bounces along, and Otto watches the sun stream through the trees. He looks at the driver and decides to make friends. "What are all those crates in the back?" he asks. The driver ignores him.

Otto turns around and sits on his knees, riding backwards. "Looks like uniforms. Boots too. Where are you taking all this stuff?"

The driver continues as if he is deaf to the boy's questions.

Otto blows through his lips. "I wish I had some water or a piece of bread."

From the vantage point of the bumpy wagon, Otto thinks the soldiers of the Red Army move far too slowly. They often stop to repair wagon wheels or check horses. The afternoon sun warms Otto and he removes his coat and muffler and holds them on his lap.

The Red Army veers to the right at a fork in the road.

"Hey, we're going the wrong way," he tells the driver. Otto looks back at the fork. "I'll have to go back to that fork to get home. Hope we stop soon. I don't want to walk forever." Otto sighs and settles, watching a horseman riding alongside the army. "I bet my Dad will be glad to see me," Otto says. "I've been gone three whole days."

The driver looks at Otto. "Three days? Where do you live?"

Otto grins. "Kovno."

"Kovno?"

"Yes. My sisters and my grandfather are going to Bremen. I'll go with my parents and grandmother."

"Bremen, eh?"

"Yup. Bremen. It's a really great place with big ships." Otto returns his attention to the back of the wagon, searching for something to talk about. "Do you know my friend Yosef Roseman? He's a soldier."

"Roseman? Where did you say you live?"

"Kovno. I live in Kovno. But we're going to Bremen."

"What's your name?"

"Otto. What's yours?"

"What's your whole name?"

"Otto Meinrel. What's yours?"

"Soldier!" yells a horseman. "What is that kid talking about?"

"Not sure, sir. Just a lot of babble."

"If he tells you where he's from, or about his family, report it to me immediately. We'll get his story tonight, one way or another. The Cheka suspects there are run-aways from some of the villages, and this might be one of them."

"Yes, sir," says the driver. Satisfied, the horseman kicks up dust along the side of the road and heads to the front of the procession.

The soldier leans to Otto. "Did you hear that? You better figure this out, kid, because I'm no fool like your friend Roseman. You want to live? Get smart. Do you see those men on the cart in front of us?" the soldier asks.

Otto looks at the black-souled men and nods.

"They're your interrogators."

"What's an interrogator?" asks Otto.

"They're the ones that will be questioning you. They hurt people. They like to hurt kids."

Otto's searches for teasing in the driver's eyes, but the driver looks serious. Otto sits back, gazing up at the trees.

"I'm really hungry," says Otto.

"There's some dried beef behind the seat, but don't let anybody see you take it," says the driver.

Otto wheedles his hand behind the seat, bringing up a large hunk — much too large to eat. He works to rip off a tiny piece and shoves the rest into his pocket. Over the next three hours bumping in the wagon, Otto studies the trees. The yellowing leaves of the birch trees shimmer translucent in the late afternoon sun. Branches are brittle in fall and require gentle coaxing to bend, taking twice as long to travel. Once bent, fall trees don't readily return to their natural stance. Anyone studying the trees would be able to follow his trail. Like these, other raiders traverse through the forest. He hasn't ridden the trees at night before. He chooses the most promising tree every few feet.

A little more than a decade before Otto's birth, a massive forest fire left millions of acres desolate. It simplified road-building for the industry-oriented political leaders, so roads were built to neighboring countries, and trade routes profited. Birch trees sprang up throughout the areas surrounding the roadways, with wide, lacy-faced ferns spreading a soft bed beneath them.

The sun lowers and the wagons halt. Otto hears ugly orders barked from everyone. The forest's beckoning tranquility contrasts sharply with the threatening chaos surrounding him. No one has loosed the dogs.

Russian children share stories of the feared hunting dogs of the Red Army. Otto and his friends played daily summer games pretending they were outsmarting the vicious animals. Otto must now play the game for real.

He slips into his coat and muffler. As the soldiers set up camp and worry about eating, Otto stays low and moves carefully, slipping from the wagon and following a well-tramped area. He ducks into the forest to the base of a choice tree and easily shimmies up the trunk to the top branches. He must get a safe distance before dark. He continues climbing upward, keeping his eye on the direction of the camp. The stiff tree requires him to climb uncomfortably high, encouraging the top to bow to its neighbor. He feels the groaning from the heart of the thin trunk and directs his weight. With his free hand he reaches wide for the next treetop, trying to spare the bend. He leaps and catches it and lets the thin branch whip him through the air, watching for the next. He sees a promising limb at the last second and leaps for it, catching it and continuing his flying from tree to tree, concentrating on each new hold and keeping the road to his left. The trees resist, having never been ridden, and he must reach for the highest, thinnest branches to get the necessary bend. Except for the air's breezy noise in his ears, Otto's movement through the treetops is silent. The trees rhythmically respond to his weight. His momentum heads away from the camp of the Red Army and back in the direction of the fork in the road. He glides from treetop to treetop, faster and faster.

For almost an hour Otto flies through the trees and the sun totally disappears from the horizon. He climbs down a few feet and rests on a branch until the moon rises, full and bright. Otto ascends back up the tree and resumes flying until they end. Otto descends to the darkness below. He doesn't want to put his feet on the ground and swings wide to land on some leaves, hoping a breeze will scatter the leaves and confuse the dogs.

In the middle of the clearing he stops and listens. He hears the distant sound of dogs barking. He scarcely breathes, the blood draining from his head and limbs. He feels faint and cannot move as the barking increases in velocity. He starts to run, but trips and falls flat on the hard, damp ground. He glances around and sees shadows everywhere. Soldiers appear behind every tree, making their way toward him. He gulps for air as he crawls and rolls toward the opposite end of the clearing, wishing he could sink into the earth. He starts to cry and yells for his parents. His voice startles him and he stays quiet, listening. He remembers his mother's soft voice. "My son, pray. Pray with the faith of your grandmother, Galayna, and whatever you need, you will receive." She had said it often, but now he is too frightened to grasp even a particle of faith. He lies in the damp, tall grass, letting the coldness of the ground penetrate his coat. He wipes his face with his sleeve and whisper-sings.

"My Lord is my refuge and my shield. My Lord, I put my hope in thy Word. Though surrounded by evil, yet shall I put my trust in Thee."

The singing slows his breathing so he sits up on his knees and looks around. He can see the moon shining through the trees, causing a dancing effect of light and shadows.

He must cross the large clearing to the next set of trees, but first he feels a need to pray. He works on his faith, and utters a prayer.

"Holy and great Father, it's me, Otto. Oh my Father, please help me to be fearless like the shepherd boy, David. I don't want to fear the dogs. I'm trying to go home. Please help me. Please show me the way."

He sits quietly waiting to feel his fear but it is gone. His mind feels clear as he considers his situation. No one at home can keep up with him when he rides the trees even if they run. The dogs sound far away and may not be the same dogs. He shudders as he remembers them charging. The moon-washed treetops are safe. He sits on his haunches, studies the sky and trees and again asks God to help him. He hears a creek and recalls a bridge they had crossed after they had taken a right turn at the fork in the road. He opts to run to the creek, thinking it would be faster than scaling another tree.

The stream is further into the trees than he thought, but he continues toward the sound. He stops at the edge of an embankment. The stream is a few feet below, and he tries to stay upright as he descends, but slides into the cold water. The fast, shallow water throws him to his side. Otto gasps, and braces himself to stand. The water tastes good. He pushes his feet into the bottom of the riverbed for added strength and rises, feeling the force of the current against his stance. He takes his time, planting each step securely before proceeding across the shallow, wide river. When he finally reaches the other embankment, he claws his way up through roots and rocks. On top, he sits for a minute before moving to the trees.

Just inside the trees he ties his muffler tight, grabs hold of the tree as high on the trunk as he can reach, pulls himself up, wraps his legs around it and climbs the trunk until he reaches the limbs. Grabbing hold he continues climbing upward until the branches thin and the tree droops. He gets his bearing and looks for a tree in the direction he needs to go and shifts his weight. Soon he is again riding the trees, flying as fast as he can under the brightness of the moon. He sees another clearing of a small village, wishing it was Kovno, but knowing it is not.

Three hours later the moon's light fades. He lowers himself to a comfortable branch and eats some jerky from his pocket. It's too dark to continue so he climbs down. Raking leaves around himself, he sleeps. Before dawn the coldness wakens him. He climbs again and waits for enough light. Throughout the day he continues flying, stopping occasionally to check for familiarity along the road. Towards evening his arms flail, almost missing their mark. His hand callouses have worn down and his right hand is bleeds. As familiar trees respond more easily, welcoming him home, his excitement overcomes the exhaustion, urging him onward.

Emerging from the forest, he drops into the familiar clearing, runs to the front door and crashes through it.

"Mom! Dad! I have so much to tell you!"

Nothing looks or feels right. His grandmother isn't sleeping on the floor mat so he quickly climbs the ladder to the bed of his parents, but it is empty, blankets and all. A panic engulfs him. He scampers down the ladder to where his grandmother sleeps and even turns her mat over. He is alone. His broken heart tells him that all of his family has left for Bremen. He takes off his shoes, climbs onto his grandmother's thin mat and cries himself to sleep.

Galayna Meinrel sits on the step of the back porch. She hasn't slept since the Cheka murdered her son, Ivan. They pushed her delicate daughter-in-law into a forced march toward a slave camp that would bring her certain death.

The old woman spent her last several nights sitting on the step of her back porch, her frenzied mind replaying the ghostly echoes from the firing squad that had extinguished her son's life. She still hears the screams, from herself and others, as they watched the mechanical Cheka riddle bullets into the bodies of their brothers, fathers and sons, many younger than Otto.

There is little chance that her husband will ever make it home again.

Even though her faith is shaken she continues her beggar's prayer, "Let me die, please let me die. There is nothing here for me. My family is gone, all gone. My husband cannot make it home. My son, my only child…gone, murdered. Please let me die." Her tears have not stopped. Her only comfort is in the peace she saw on the face of her angelic son as he faced the firing squad. He knew his children were safe. She saw the same peace in the face of Fedora when they led her away.

Galayna mourns that the Cheka adjudged her too old to waste a bullet. She tried to join Fedora in the march to the slave camp, thinking she could somehow share the burden. A young soldier knocked her away. She begged him to take her or to shoot her, but instead he struck her senseless and left her for dead.

When she was able, she sat up, the mute scenes around her seeming to move in slow motion. A toddler stood by the lifeless body of the rabbi, fascinated by the blood oozing onto her foot from his mouth. A mother who had been spared was grasping her dead son and wailing, although Galayna could not hear it. Another child walked in circles, crying, not knowing where to go. They toppled the town's windmill and trampled productive gardens. Just beyond that she could see where the corpses were laying from the executions. Old women moved bodies and, from the look on their faces, wept; but Galayna's world was silent. She laid her bloodied head back on the earth, willing it to swallow her.

It was dark when she regained consciousness. Burning fires cast light on the town square. She heard hoarse cries from villagers and scrapes from shovels. She stood erect and forced her body to the carcasses of the men and boys.

When she found Ivan, she worked to loosen him from his fallen comrades, and pulled him by his legs to the edge of the heap. She thought for a moment that she could pick him up in her arms and carry him home, but she could not. She put her body between his legs, grabbed him at the knees, and dragged him home. His arms, head and back made a dragging sound against the ground, and she missed her deafness. She laid him out beside the back porch, and went into the house.

The house was intact. Prior to the raid, she had helped Fedora and Ivan move blankets, mats and dishes underneath the house. Most of the family's possessions — anything that could be sold for ship's passage—was on the wagon bound for Germany. Perhaps the Cheka had glanced inside and thought the home had already been sacked. She lifted the floorboards and climbed under the house. She brought up a shovel, a pick, and blanket. She walked to the area behind the empty chicken pen and dug a grave in the stony earth. She dug until daylight, and dragged her son's body to the edge of the grave and wrapped it. Before she covered his face, she dropped to her knees and held it on her lap. She smoothed his hair, wailed, covered his face, and rolled him into the earth. Thud.

Now, five days later, she shudders as she recalls the sound. Thud. She forces her mind away from it. Her thoughts reach for Fedora and she wonders what might be happening to her. She drops the shawl from her shoulders, trying to feel as cold as Fedora. Finally, she stands to enter her very empty house, where she will kneel at her bed and beg God again to end her life.

Galayna had not heard Otto enter the home, nor had she heard him cry. Her feelings are both joyous and foreboding to find him asleep on her bed. What could have happened to her dear husband and darling granddaughters? And why is her beloved little redhead here, looking so dirty, torn and thin? She lets him sleep. In the morning they will share information of their loved ones. She lies down beside him and covers him with her shawl. For the first time since the Cheka's murdering rampage, Galayna sleeps.

# CHAPTER 12
## *Fall 1920*

The next morning dawns clear and cold. Otto's grandmother ignores his questions about his parents. She helps him bathe and makes him a glorious breakfast of seed potatoes. He devours every bite. After they do a few chores, Galayna brings her grandson into the house and sits across from him at the kitchen table. Her hair hangs in gray clumps and her features droop.

"When was the last time you saw your grandfather? Where are Chana and Amalie?"

"The Red Army was coming on the road. Grandfather hid Chana, Amalie and the wagon and he picked me up and ran under a bridge. He can run really fast." Otto recounts how he had to push his grandfather out of the way and run up the embankment. He describes the vicious dogs and makes rafter-shaking growling noises. He tells her of the soldier picking him up just as the dogs were ready to eat him, and about the ugly men on the wagon. Finally he talks of flying through the trees until his arms ached, and of finding empty beds at home. "Where is mother? She should be here. Did she and Papa go to Bremen?"

"Otto, your father was killed. I'm so sorry. The Cheka shot him. I was digging his grave when you came home last night." Otto's happy face breaks into objections, then tears, then wailing.

"No! Papa! I want Papa!" he cries. "Where is my mother?" he sobs.

"They took her to a slave camp, Otto. She will die there."

"No! Mama!"

"Can I tell you about your Father, Otto? Can I tell you how happy he was when he died, knowing his children were safe?"

Otto yowls and tries to cover his ears, but his grandmother moves his hands and says all the horrible words. When she finishes she leads her hysterical grandson back to bed and lies down with him, holding him close and letting him convulse and object in her arms. At dinnertime, she fixes a tray of simple bread and water. Galayna tells him stories of happier times.

Otto cannot hold his aching inside, and he bursts into loud, anguished objections. His grandmother removes the tray and allows him to howl until he falls asleep.

When Otto awakens the next morning, the pain of the previous day's news fills him and he cries. He wants to go back to sleep and shut it out, but his grandmother tells him to dress and do chores.

Otto forces himself to sit up and put on his pants and button his shirt. He walks outside barefooted, wanting to be obedient to his grandmother. The frosted ground grips him. All the trees have dropped their leaves. Nothing looks or feels the same to him. He looks at the trampled garden and broken, empty animal pens. The neighbor's doors and windows are broken and clothing and broken furniture are strewn everywhere. Otto looks around cogitating what the routine of his chores should be. There are no chickens or eggs. There are no animals to feed or vegetables to harvest. His eyes settle on the empty chicken coup. He bundles branches together to use as a broom and sweeps out the pen. He walks to the garden area where fresh soil indicates his father's grave. When he thinks of his father lying in the cold ground, he sits down hard on the dirt and howls again, not caring who hears him.

Galayna sits beside him, bringing his head to her lap. "Howl, grandson. Howl and yell and cry to God. Mourn your heart." Otto continues his rants, increasing in volume. "They have taken your father and mother. Cry for them, grandson. Cry until all your tears are gone." Otto complies. When he stops Galayna lifts him onto her lap and holds him close. He wants to fall asleep against her body.

"Let's go into the house, Otto." She stands him up and pushes herself to her feet. Inside, she doesn't bother to close the door. He watches her move about, packing a knapsack.

"It's dangerous for you here, Otto." she says. "Other grandmothers buried their grandsons and feel our family is at fault because we aided Fanya and she shot Lenin. I must get you to a safe place."

Otto sits in numb silence.

"We're in a predicament, grandson. We have no friends here—all the boys are dead, and they blame us. You weren't here so you are the only boy in all of Kovno, and they will be angry when they see you."

"My friends? They killed my friends?"

"Yes. They shot all the males old enough to stand. Your mother and father were wise to send you and your sisters away. But now you're in danger. I can't let them find you."

"I could live in the cellar," Otto offers.

"No, you would be discovered. I have a half-sister. Remember me talking of your Aunt Vyvyan?"

"No."

"After my mother died my father remarried a younger woman and they had a child, my half-sister, Vyvyan. She's thirty years younger than me, but when I went to my father's funeral I met her. She was twelve by then and I was forty-two. Even though we were decades apart, Vyvyan was gracious and we found common interests and traits. We shared memories and feelings about our father and we felt close to one another. We corresponded regularly until just before her marriage. I haven't heard from her for several years—not since before her wedding. She's thirty now."

"I don't know her."

"We're going to her house."

"Where does she live?"

"Rostov."

"Does she have kids?"

"I don't think so. She would have told me. Her husband is very influential." Galayna stops her preparations and touches Otto's shoulder, stooping to look into his eyes.

"Otto, I am praying this will give you a chance. It is all I have left to give you—a chance. I don't know what we will find at your Aunt Vyvyan's, but I have to try."

"All right, Grandmother." Otto hugs her.

"Grandmother, where is my mother's slave camp?"

"Why would you want to know, Otto?"

"I can save her. I'll show her how to climb trees and we could get away—like I got away from the Red Army."

"No, Otto. She cannot be saved. No one knows where the slave camp is, just that it's in the icy north, hundreds and hundreds of miles from here where there are no trees—just snow and ice."

"Well, maybe…"

"No, Otto. It isn't your worry to find your mother. That worry belongs to me and your grandfather."

"But I have to find her," he says. "I have to."

"Don't you understand the sacrifice of your parents? It gave them peace to save your life. They knew they would die but they were happy because their children were safe. You must honor her final sacrifice and stay alive. She could not bear it if she knew you were in danger."

"So, if it's your job to find her, what if you can't?"

"We probably won't be able to, but if she is to be found, your grandfather and I will find her. Come now, Otto. We have a long walk ahead. Without your hat you will need to wrap your muffler around your head."


GALAYNA'S SWIFT, STEADY pace requires Otto to run to keep up with her.

"Grandmother, did my mother walk this way?"

"No. We are walking east. They went northwest."

"Did she take food?"

"No."

"Was she wearing her warm coat?"

"Yes. Otto, we aren't going to talk of your mother any more today. Keep up, grandson."

After sundown, Galayna and Otto hide behind a barn and sleep close together in a pile of leaves. Before dawn Galayna shakes Otto awake.

"Sh. Quiet, Otto. We need to get going."

Again Galayna sets the pace and Otto lags behind, distracted by bugs, rocks, sticks and trees. Shortly after dawn Otto runs to catch up with her and she hands him a slice of a seed potato.

"Grandmother," he says. "Yosef can help me find my mother."

"No, Otto."

"But he found Fanya. It took him years but…"

Galayna turns and grabs Otto's shoulders and stoops down.

"Otto, you must never mention Fanya. Or Yosef."

"But why, Grandmother? He can find anybody."

Galayna keeps her voice low even though no one is close. "Fanya was shot. It is because we helped her that the Cheka came to Kovno. It is because of Fanya that your sisters and Grandfather had to leave Kovno. If you speak of Fanya or Yosef it will surely bring you death. Don't talk of them again."

Otto throws down his stick and sits on the ground. Galayna sighs and walks back to him.

"See those boys running through the trees?" She says pointing to the treeline.

"Yes," Otto answers.

"If they don't rob from people they'll starve. The only reason they haven't accosted us is because we're moving steady and we look thinner than they are. If we stop, they'll come after us. We can't stop again."

"What about that grandma carrying the child?" asks Otto, pointing to a woman rocking a baby.

"They'll be in trouble before long," says Galayna. "No more dawdling." Galayna walks fast and Otto runs to keep up.


THE EVENING OF the third day the forlorn twosome reaches the enclosed porch of Vyvyan's home in Rostov. They open the gate, walk through the courtyard and up the stoop and Galayna bangs on the door, Vyvyan opens it almost immediately, and Otto beholds his great aunt for the first time.

Aunt Vyvyan, tall and slender, wears a white poet blouse, black suede weskit and deep red silk skirt with black vertical suede stripes. Her dark brown braids twirl around her head, and she smells like fresh flowers. Everything about her reminds Otto of a youthful version of his grandmother, and he realizes that his grandmother may have been a beautiful woman.

His aunt looks at Galayna, trying to focus. "Galayna!" she gasps at last, kissing her sister. "Come in," she stutters apologetically.

Their provisions ran out the evening before and Otto wants to enter and eat whatever she offers, but his grandmother's hand stops him. "You must sit here on the porch for a short while," she tells him.

"Oh, Galayna—your grandson?"

"Yes," Galayna answers.

The two women go inside and shut the door. Otto sits on the front steps. An hour before, he and his grandmother heard distant bells and talked of the wonder of them. Now the bells ring again. They sound close by, and Otto walks to the edge of the porch to look for them. A grand cathedral sits across the valley and he sees swaying bells in the towers. He listens in rapture as large, pealing bongs bounce across buildings and hillsides, followed closely by stridently pitched higher clangs of hypnotic patterns and tones. The peeling sounds continue for half an hour, filling the air with magic. When they finish, he looks at Aunt Vyvyan's closed door and blows through his lips. He walks back to the steps and plunks down, trying to re-create the sounds of the bells. He walks the courtyard, searching for rocks and sticks and returns to the steps, empty-handed. The door opens.

"Come in, lad," says Aunt Vyvyan.

He looks around the house. The large entry could swallow his entire home. He stares at the crystal candelabra, not noticing his great aunt studying him.

She touches his hair.

"I know what to do," she tells Galayna. She places her hand gently under Otto's chin and meets his blue eyes with her black. "Otto, you will be staying here with me. Your grandmother must go back to Kovno to wait for your grandfather. Your parents are not able to raise you, and your grandmother cannot keep you in

Kovno. So, you are to be my son. Do you understand what it means when I say you are to be my son?"

Otto gazes into her dark eyes, watching the words fall from her soft lips, but resisting the ideas she tries to form in his head. She is so fresh and bright; he feels almost a reverence peering into the moist eyes of his great aunt. He tilts his head.

"I do not know how to be anything but a son," he whispers. "And that means that I must find my mother."

Vyvyan fully embraces the dirty lad. She kisses him on the forehead and on the cheek, and bids him to join his grandmother on the sofa.

Vyvyan walks into her kitchen and brings back a tray of cakes and tea. Otto watches his grandmother keep her ravenous appetite in check and obey the proprieties of graciousness, eating each bite of cake only after her hostess takes a bite. He tries to do the same, but cannot resist eating a little faster than Aunt Vyvyan, and asks for seconds before they are offered. Vyvyan's eyes widen.

"Please, Galayna, forgive me. Come into my kitchen. I have food that will sustain us for weeks." She takes their hands, leads them into her kitchen and sits them at her table. She pulls cold chicken, sausages, boiled eggs, apples, bread and milk from her pantry.

"Come, Otto," she says. "Fill your plate with anything you want."

Otto's eyebrows arch. "Anything?" he asks.

Vyvyan laughs. "Let me help you. Do you like boiled eggs?" She fills his plate, sets it in front of him, and turns to prepare Vyvyan's plate.

"Please, no, Vyvyan, it's far too much," says Galayna. "We aren't accustomed to eating very much. Just give me a plate so I can share with Otto."

Vyvyan gives Galayna a plate and pours herself a cup of tea, and sits at the table to watch them eat, discussing the delectable food. After a few bites Otto holds his stomach and rolls his eyes.

"Just eat what you can," says Vyvyan. "You don't have to clean your plate."

Otto looks at his grandmother.

"It's all right, Otto," Galayna says. "You're Vyvyan's son now. You can do what she tells you."

"Maybe a little more," says Otto, picking up an apple slice.

Vyvyan sips her tea. "I thought of coming to you many times, Galayna. After mother died last year, you're the one I needed but I didn't want to impose on your beautiful family." Galayna reaches for her sister's hand and kisses it. Vyvyan continues. "I've felt deep loneliness here. I'm sorry that your tragedy will turn into my joy."

"It will also be my joy if you succeed. This little one is very open and always filled with wonderment. Your task will not be an easy one, I fear," Galayna says.

Vyvyan carries her cup to the basin, pulls a large galvanized tub from the corner of the kitchen, pours hot water from the kettle into the tub, refills the kettle and returns it to the stove. By the time Galayna and Otto finish eating, the tub has enough warm water, and they take turns bathing. Vyvyan dresses Otto in a clean nightshirt and gives Galayna a soft nightdress. She takes Otto's hand and leads him upstairs to a guest bedroom. Otto falls asleep almost before his head sinks into the down of the pillow.

# CHAPTER 13

## *October 1920*

Galayna and Vyvyan awake simultaneously in the pre-dawn. As they dress, Galayna finds Vyvyan's dark blue dress in place of her black one. After Vyvyan coaxes her into it, they braid one another's hair. Vyvyan hungers for stories of her father, which Galayna generously supplies, answering each of Vyvyan's questions in detail.

"I must tell you about my husband, Anatoly," Vyvyan levels in even, lifeless words. Her eyes train downward as she pours their tea, and hints of crimson singe her cheeks. She takes a deep breath and blows it out slowly. She lifts her teacup to her lips, sips, and gently sets it back on its dish. She raises her head and looks into Galayna's face. Galayna notices her eyelids drop slightly and moisture brim in their depths.

"I can see you're not a fragile woman, dearest sister," says Galayna. "Please, tell me of your husband."

"My mother's husband, Ilya, was a wretched step-father. He arranged for me to marry Anatoly. I didn't know anything about it for many years and couldn't figure out why the powerful Anatoly Kazakov would want to marry a gangly child like me. In any case, Anatoly was nothing more than one of my father's business associates and I had no interest in marrying him.

"When I was nineteen, I met a wonderful man — a pilot, Alexander. I loved Alexander and I know he loved me." Vyvyan tilts her head slightly back and her words soften. "My Alexander was fearless. He took me up into the clouds once. I tried not to tell my mother about it, but it was too wonderful — impossible not to share. My mother was happy for me and we laughed about it, but she was also afraid for me. It was then that she told me of my arranged marriage to Anatoly. I told her I couldn't marry anyone except Alexander. I refused to stop loving him.

"When Anatoly came for a visit I told him, in front of my stepfather, that I loved Alexander and would never love anyone else. Anatoly had no interest in my love affair, or even in love for that matter. He had a bargain with my step-father." Vyvyan's voice shakes and her pitch rises. She sips her tea and it down, looking into Galayna's eyes. "Alexander had German blood as well. His hair was auburn colored—not red like Otto's but reddish enough. The timing is right for Otto to be my son."

Galayna's puts her hand on her heart.

Vyvyan continues, "My Anatoly is greatly loved by the people. He speaks with conviction and persuasion. They seem to think his clumsiness is endearing, but here, with me, Anatoly is like a cold machine. His heart has no life. His conversation is barely functional. He thought my mother's husband was my real father, and, for my mother's sake, I had to accept that insult.

"My step-father was a brutal man, particularly to my mother. Masquerading as his daughter, I have value to Anatoly. If he knew the truth I fear he would have had me dispatched long ago. Anatoly has dark energy. He was there when Alexander's plane crashed. He came home that night, I poured his coffee, and he had no compunction about telling me, right there, that my beautiful Alexander had died in a fiery crash, just as someone might talk of the weather. My Alexander – dead – and his death spewed through the mouth of someone incapable of natural feelings. It was as though my life had been jerked from my breast." Hot tears drop on her cheeks and she dries her face.

106

"Galayna, I do not know how Anatoly will respond to having Otto here. He will easily believe that Otto is my son by Alexander." She looks at Galayna, fear apparent on her face. "Otto and I may both be joining Fedora in the slave camp."

Galayna studies her sister. She draws her spoon from her teacup and dries it in her mouth, then loosely holds the handle of the spoon and shakes it at Vyvyan as she talks.

"My Otto will be protected, Vyvyan. With grace, Ivan and his beautiful Fedora helped their children slip out of Kovno, just minutes before the bloody Cheka came. They would have shot Otto alongside his father. Otto saved his sisters by averting attention away from them. Dogs attacked him and he was plucked from harm's way. The Red Army took him prisoner and he escaped by flying through the tops of trees. Otto was completely lost in a foreign place and yet he found his way home. I did not know if you would accept him when we came, but you are willing to take him into your bosom as dearly as if he were your own son, and you are willing to share him with the memory of your beloved Alexander. It is God's will that my grandson be protected. Anatoly with all his evil is no match for the will of God. You watch, dear sister, and learn of God."

Vyvyan smiles, her tension dispelled. Galayna lays down her spoon and places her forearms on the table, offering her hands to Vyvyan. Vyvyan encloses her soft hands around her sister's rough ones.

"Thank you, Vyvyan. You have a good, generous heart. My grandson will prosper under your care."

Galayna rises and walks to the corner where her old black dress is draped on the drying rack. She slips it over the top of her new blue one. Vyvyan helps Galayna place cheeses and dried fruits into the loose folds of the black dress. Galayna must appear poorer than any of the hooligans roaming the countryside on her long, lonely walk home.

Galayna climbs the stairs to say good-bye to her beloved grandson. She enters the bedroom where Otto is sleeping, sits on the bed and runs her fingers through the locks of his red curls.

"Otto, my Otto. Awake and say goodbye to your grandmother. I must go back and await your grandfather."

Otto sits up too quickly. "No!" he says, kicking off the covers. "I'm going with you."

"No, grandson," she says. "You must stay here."

Otto stiffins and protests.

Galayna slips her scarf over her head and kneels beside the bed. "Otto, I'm going to pray now. This is a prayer straight to God's ear and it is about you. You must remember every word it."

Otto sniffs. "All right." He slips off the bed onto his knees beside his grandmother.

"Oh God in Heaven who parted the seas and watched over the boy Joseph. It is me, Galayna. Oh God who hears my prayers, please hear this one that I offer with all my heart for my little grandson who is kneeling here beside me. I know that you love Otto just as you loved the boy Joseph in Egypt. Otto's father is dead. His mother is a prisoner and Otto wants to find her. It would be dangerous for him to look for her. Otto doesn't understand about slave prisons. I beg of thee, dearest God, please send Otto a dream so he will see the death of his mother. If he sees her death he will accept it, so please show it to him.

"I must leave Otto in this house to be raised by my sister Vyvyan. Help Otto to carefully obey her.

"Help him to pray to thee always, even if he must pray secretly.

"When he is a man, please help him to find his sisters.

"Thank you, dear God, for hearing my prayer. Amen."

Otto sobs. Galayna lifts him into bed and sits beside him.

"Please don't leave me, Grandmother."

"It's okay to cry," Galayna says wiping her own tears. "Did you hear the words of my prayer?"

"Yes, but I don't want to stay here. I just want my mother."

"You must remember all the words of my prayer. Promise me that you will obey all that your Aunt Vyvyan tells you, no matter how difficult. When you are a man, you must find your sisters. Give me your word that you will do as I ask."

Otto can hardly speak past the swelling lump in his throat. "Grandmother. Please. Please don't make me promise."

"Otto, tell me what you will do."

"My mother cannot die!" he exclaims, sitting upright and slamming his hands on the bed.

"Yes, Otto. She will die and you will be told by God when she does. All you can do, dear grandson, is obey her last wish— you must be safe. Now promise me that you will grow up in this house and obey your Aunt Vyvyan. And when you are a man you will go and find your sisters."

Otto cries harder.

"I need to hear the words, Otto," Galayna says, raising her voice. "Give me your word!"

The little boy's chest heaves and his words come out in half syllables. Through coughs and sobs he makes the promises required. "I will obey Aunt Vyvyan, and I will grow up, and I will find my sisters."

"Good, my darling. Now, lie back down and do not get up until I am gone." He throws himself back on the bed wailing. She tucks the covers around his shoulders, gazes at his sorrowful face and kisses his forehead. She arises quickly, walks from the room and descends the stairs.

Otto slows his wailing to a sobbing plea "No, don't go, please don't go," and he listens for her voice. She says a few words to his aunt, and then the front door opens and closes. He buries his face into depths of his pillow and screams.

# CHAPTER 14

## *October 1920*

Vyvyan watches her sister walk away. As Galayna disappears around a building, Vyvyan's heart warms. Her son lies in the bed upstairs. She places some fruit and milk on a tray and walks up to Otto's room and sits on a chair beside his bed. She fishes him out of the covers, wipes his tears and helps him sit up. He sucks air involuntarily from his sobbing. He shies away from the tray, and she sets it on the bed beside him. She wishes she could allow him time to adjust, but she cannot.

"Otto, I want to have a special bond with you," she says. "I want us to always tell the truth to one another, agreed?"

Otto looks around for a hanky and sees a huge covering on his pillow. He wrestles with it to try to release the pillow. Vyvyan watches his curious struggle to liberate the pillow and lends a hand. When the case is free, Otto rolls it into a ball, buries his face into it and blows loudly. Vyvyan jumps. Otto finishes the job of wiping his nose and face.

"I will always tell you the truth," he says.

Vyvyan almost smiles, and proceeds with the serious task at hand. "Otto, you and I will share some secrets that no one else except your grandmother will know about. I have to trust you, and you have to trust me."

Otto looks up into her eyes with growing wonder, handing her the pillowcase. Vyvyan uses the pillowcase to softly wipe moisture from his dark lashes.

"Your grandmother took a risk coming here," she explains. "My husband is a cruel and powerful man. Do you remember the Red Army that took you prisoner – the army that even your brave grandfather feared?"

"Yes."

"My husband gives them orders, and they obey him."

"He does?"

"Yes. And many other things even more powerful than that. You and I must make him believe that you are my son. If he thinks you have another mother, he will punish you and me, and will use the Red Army to hurt your mother and grandmother."

Otto's breathing increases.

"I'm sorry to have to explain this to you," she says. "My home is not a safe place, and I can't soften the fear."

"I know about keeping secrets," he says. "My mother said not to tell my friends about going to Bremen and I didn't tell them."

Vyvyan smiles. "It sounds like you are a very good secret-keeper."

"I am," he says.

"That is good," Vyvyan pets his cheek with the back of her finger. "The most important part of our secret is to remember that you are my son, and no one else's."

Otto breaks his gaze from hers. He finds a loose thread on the blanket and twists it around his finger.

"Perhaps I need to build our story a little slower," says Vyvyan. "I would like to know more about your mother. Is she pretty?"

Otto doesn't hesitate and raises his deep blue eyes to Vyvyan. "She's really pretty."

"Does she like to read to you?"

"Every day. And I read to her."

For the next hour Vyvyan learns about Fedora. When Otto pauses, she rakes her fingers through his thick curls like his mother. "Otto, you and I will do many things just like your mother. That way, when you join her again, she will see that you are a strong and wise son." Otto nods. "But until she returns, I will be your mother."

"You smell good, like my mother. You are pretty, and so is my mother." He takes a deep breath and blows it out. "I think you will be a very good mother."

Vyvyan cannot hold back any longer. She pulls him to her, kissing him all over his face. "My sweet, handsome son," she laughs.

"If you are my mother, what should I call you?" Otto asks.

"Can you call me mother?"

"Of course, mother," grins Otto, loving all the kisses. "I called my real mama, mama, so I can call you mother."

Vyvyan giggles and Otto lays against her.

"Very well, my darling son," she says, holding him at arm's length. "You look just like my son, but I'll need to cut your hair a little."

"Mama likes my curls," Otto says.

"We'll leave some of them," Vyvyan says. "Now, we need to talk about your father."

Otto's tears surface and Vyvyan hands him the pillowcase.

"Your father must have been a very good man," Vyvyan says.

Otto nods, his chin quivering.

"You must help me know what your father taught you about being a man. You and I will figure out what was important to him, and you will be the kind of man that he would want you to be."

"My Father likes me to tell the truth," Otto says.

"We will always tell the truth to each other, and to your grandmother," says Vyvyan. "What is the last thing your father told you?"

"To take care of my sisters," Otto says.

"And you did," says Vyvyan. "It would have made him very proud. Now we must also take care of your mother and grandmother, which will require us to keep big secrets."

"What kind of secrets?" asks Otto.

"You must make my husband think you are my son, and never let anyone know about your real mother or grandmother," says Vyvyan.

"But what about mama?" asks Otto. "We need to find her."

"Your grandmother will try to find your mother, but it is very important that you never speak of her or your father, or anyone else in your family. Sometimes, when we are all alone like we are right now, I will ask you questions about them and then you will know it is safe to talk about them, but otherwise you must never mention them out loud again – and you must never mention the name Meinrel. From now on you are only Otto. If Anatoly does not give you his name, I will think of another name, but you will never say Meinrel again."

"Why?" asks Otto.

Vyvyan repeats the information. "Otto, it is very dangerous. Anatoly must never, never know about your real family. If he asks you your name it is just plain Otto, never Otto Meinrel. Over the next several days we will practice our secrets. I will try to trick you, but you will be far too clever to be tricked." She studies him for a minute. "What is your name, boy," she queries, dropping her voice to a lower pitch.

Otto reaches for a piece of fruit and pops it into his mouth. "Otto!" he declares. "Just plain Otto."

Vyvyan laughs.

# CHAPTER 15
## *November 1920*

Anatoly Kazakov steps from the carriage and waves off the driver. It has been a long and difficult trip to Moscow, and he has not gained the support he needs. He must be closer to Vladimir Lenin. He will find an apartment in Moscow and move Vyvyan there. She has adequate majesty and charm to attract the right social circles of Moscow, and, as much as he detests pomp, it is finally necessary. But will she try to be charming? This he cannot control, and it irritates him. He steps to the front door and opens it. Vyvyan is there immediately to tend to his coat and suitcase. He follows her into the kitchen, and sees a red-haired boy-child writing on a hand-held chalkboard.

"Anatoly, this is my son, Otto. Otto, this is my husband, Anatoly."

Anatoly glares at Otto without expression.

Vyvyan begins her well-rehearsed explanation. "I'm sure father told you of Otto. I had not known where father placed him until this week when a peasant woman brought him to me. The country is starving, and they can no longer care for him."

Anatoly drops down hard in a chair across from the boy, staring at the lad. Vyvyan immediately sets a plate of his favorite food in front of him, and Anatoly's mind whirs. Ilya had said nothing about this boy, who must have been born around the time he had married Vyvyan. That would have been easily disguised, since he had been away for months prior to their marriage. He was well aware of Vyvyan's lover, the pilot.

Anatoly and Otto stare at one another. Anatoly shoves food into his mouth, knowing that sounds inside his mouth fill the silence.

Otto turns his attention to writing Russian letters on his chalk board. His chalk screeches against the chalkboard but Otto ignores it, working with increased diligence, shaping the letters more deliberately with each screech.

The hair stands up on the back of Anatoly's neck.

"Come, Otto, you must get ready for bed," Vyvyan says, taking his chalk.

Even for a child it is far too early for bed but Otto takes Vyvyan's hand and obediently ascends the stairs.

When Vyvyan returns to the kitchen she scoops a large piece of cake onto a plate, pours a glass of rich cream, and sets them before Anatoly.

"You haven't baked for quite some time," he says, smacking the cake and gulping the milk. He stretches as she washes the plate and glass, rises and walks up the stairs. She follows him without being told. Anatoly smiles.


ANATOLY AWAKENS BEFORE dawn and hears Vyvyan in the kitchen preparing food. The smell of fresh bread fills the house. He dresses and descends the stairs.

"I will acknowledge the child as my son," he says. "He will be known as Otto Kazakov. There can be no question."

"Yes, Anatoly." She slices his bread. "I will teach Otto that he is your son. There will be no question."

"We will be relocating to Moscow in spring," he says. "I will arrange a house."

"Yes, Anatoly."

"Otto will be enrolled as a Young Pioneer in the school of sciences. As Minister of Education it will be expected that my son excels academically. I will not be embarrassed by him."

"Yes, Anatoly. He will excel."

"You will order his uniforms today. You must assure that he is tutored properly. I will arrange for the books he must master."

"Yes, Anatoly."

Anatoly allows her to fuss over him. Fate has finally given him a pawn to control Vyvyan—her son. She will be as charming as he requires. The social circles of Moscow will be impressed with his family.

# CHAPTER 16
## *November 1920*

Chingas leans on the mare for balance. His leg needs wrapping again.

"Look, girls!" he says, pointing to a sign. "We made it to Zbaraz, Galacia. That means we're out of Russia."

"I hope we won't be running into the Red Army anymore," says Chana. "They seem to be everywhere."

It's getting pretty late." Amalie says.

"There's a burned-out castle up ahead," Chingas says. "We'll stay there. If I remember right it's a short climb but well worth it. Look for firewood."

"I've been picking up sticks all day," says Chana. "All we need is a big log."

"Here's the hill," says Chingas. "There are more rocks than I remember."

"Grandfather, there are rock walls, every few meters all the way to the top," says Chana.

"Aye. It used to be so easy when I was young. I'll never get the wagon up there," Chingas says.

"Do you think there's another way up?" asks Amalie.

"I don't remember," says Chingas. "It's been twenty years. The castle looks the same."

The evening sun silhouettes the immense ancient stone structure. On the left, a wide, flat-topped turret rises higher than the rest of the building. On the right, a tall rectangular shape juts forward. The central area covers fifty meters across and fifty meters high, with large arched window openings from three levels.

"We'll run up and see if we can find another route," says Chana. "It's a very good place, Grandfather."

Chingas watches Chana and Amalie climb, hoisting and pulling one another over rocks and walls, occasionally disappearing into gullies. The last wall is the highest. The sun sinks down the horizon.

Chingas waits, straining his eye in the twilight. Large white flakes drift downward, obscuring his ability to see his granddaughters. He moves his head forward, squinting, and sees movement midway down the hill. Chana has her skirt hiked, jumping down from rocks and running across open spaces, Amalie right behind her.

Chana is breathless. "Soldiers. They're at the castle. Maybe the Red Army."

"Quickly, girls," says Chingas. He swats the mare and grips her bridle, allowing the horse to pull him along. They lumber for several minutes before they see an obscured trail and follow it off the road. The trail opens to a grove of trees and they huddle together near the horse, breathing hard as the large white flakes drop faster. Darkness falls but the white snow keeps the area bright enough to see. Chingas convulses with chill spasms. Chana and Amalie put their arms around him but his spasms continue.

"Grandfather, I see a light through the trees," whispers Amalie.

"I don't see anything," Chingas's says shakily.

"It's further down this trail, Grandfather. You can see it through there."

"Yes, Amalie. I think it's a light," says Chana. I can find my way down this path to get a closer look."

"Go together," says Chingas. "Hold onto each other. Mark your way with Chana's sticks. The snow will cover your steps."

Chana reaches for a quilt inside the wagon and wraps it around Chingas's shoulders. "We'll be right back, Grandfather."

Chingas's leg, numb and swollen, has quit throbbing. The horse supports him.

Chingas watches them disappear and talks to himself. "Go ahead, granddaughters. I fear I'm finished." Chingas looks at the old mare. "Thanks, old friend. Thanks for letting me lean on you." Chingas looks up at the falling snowflakes, removes his hat and closes his eye.

"God, I am Galayna's husband, Chingas. I haven't talked to you for a while. I've been so ashamed since I lost my precious grandson, Otto. I hope you are there. Galayna says you are and she doesn't lie.

"Remember the promise you made Galayna? She said you would help me get the children to Bremen. We're not halfway there yet and I'm finished, worn out, decrepit, barely in Galacia with these two young women. I must protect them. I'm down to one eye and one leg and not much else. I'm so very weak. Please, I beg you, give me the strength to get Chana and Amalie safely to Bremen. Galayna said it wasn't hard for you, seeing that you parted the Red Sea."

"Who are you talking to, Grandfather?" asks Chana.

Chingas shakes the snow from his face. "Your grandmother's God," Chingas answers.

"Come, Grandfather. We have a place to stay and the family has dinner waiting for us."

Chingas grips the bridle and pats the mare forward.

THE BUSTLING SOUNDS inside the house awaken Chingas. "Chana," he calls, arising. Chana runs to his side. "How did I get here? I don't remember."

"You collapsed, Grandfather. We all helped you get here."

"The mare?" he asks.

"In a comfortable barn, eating hay," says Chana.

"What time is it?"

"Almost dinner time."

"Dinner?"

"Yes. I was able to spoon a few bites into you last evening but you've been sleeping since we arrived last night."

Chingas sees his hosts watching him and feels embarrassed. "I'm sorry to have taken up your floor," he says. "Thank you for helping us."

Chana translates her grandfather's words into Russian and the couple smiles and nods at Chingas, speaking phrases to Chana.

"They say it's good that you found them when you did," she says. "It's been stormy all day, Grandfather. We wouldn't have gotten very far. Grandfather, let me introduce you to Daniel and Coco Wozniak."

The Wozniaks are in their late forties. Coco Wozniak, short and rotund, wears a kerchief on her head to hide her thinning hair. Her floor-length, blue cotton dress has a belted waist somewhere underneath her ample bust. Her eyes twinkle when she smiles. Daniel Wozniak's powerful build, tall and muscle-bound, reminds Chingas of Ivan. Daniel's light brown hair, balding on top, hangs in wisps around his ears. His roomy white shirt, pleated across the shoulders, hangs loose over his pants. His serious hazel eyes look genuinely concerned.

The men shake hands and Daniel Wozniak says something.

"He says he is sorry about Otto," translates Chana as Daniel continues to talk. "He also says that he lost his son and understands why your body broke down and that he's glad it broke down at his door. He says we can stay as long as we wish."

Chingas sniffs back sudden tears.

"I think I have everything on the table for dinner," says Amalie. She talks with Coco Wosniak and Coco motions to Chingas. Chana and Daniel haul Chingas to his feet and support his weight. He hobbles to the table and sits. The Wozniak's join hands and each take hold of Chana and Amalie's hands. Chana and Amalie join hands with Chingas. Mrs. Wozniak says a lengthy prayer, at the end of which Mr. Wozniak says "Amen." They pass food to their guests. Amalie and Coco take turns chatting, Coco often giggling.

"I told them our mother is Russian," says Amalie.

"I can speak a little Russian," says Chingas. "This doesn't sound like Russian."

"Many of the words are similar," says Amalie. "Try listening like you know what they're saying and you'll catch it. It's more like a different slant on the same words mother used."

Chingas shakes his head. "You mean to tell me that while I slept you two learned a whole new language?" Amalie pats his arm and smiles.

Chingas looks around. The house is quadruple the size of their home in Kovno, with a steep staircase serving a spacious upper level that appears partitioned into rooms. The center of the ceiling is a full two stories high, maybe more. An indoor fireplace keeps the home cozy and provides for cooking. A work surface runs the length of the wall next to their table, with crisp yellow curtains dropping from the work surface almost to the floor. Chingas sees the base of barrels and boxes stored behind the curtains. The window above the work surface reveals falling snow and darkening skies. On either side of the window guns hang on the wall.

"Chingas," Daniel says. "I lead the Polish Riflemen's Association. I teach many young soldiers to shoot."

Chana begins to translate but Chingas stops her. "I think I understand," Chingas says. "Did Daniel shoot a lot of young soldiers?"

"No, Grandfather. He said he teaches young soldiers to shoot," says Chana.

"There are over three thousand local branches of the Riflemen's Association, each one with over two hundred members," says Daniel. "I can guarantee your safety while you're here."

"I understood that," says Chingas. "Daniel has access to about 60,000 volunteers who know how to shoot and they all have guns. He says he can protect us." Chingas changes his German to broken Russian, addressing Daniel. "It's been so long since I've felt safe. If we had such groups in Russia we could defend ourselves. Having a Riflemen's Association is something I have fantasized about, but in Russia they disarmed us long ago, one village at a time. Now only the bullies and thugs in uniform have guns."

"Chana and Amalie helped me clean my guns today," Daniel says. I didn't have oil so we used some of yours."

"Good!" says Chingas, eating a piece of bread. A wave of exhaustion causes Chingas to grab the edge of the table. "Mrs. Wozniak, you have prepared an amazing feast, and I am truly grateful. Fresh meat, bread, potatoes and beans. I regret I only have the energy to eat a little bread. Would you kindly excuse me?"

"Your beautiful granddaughters did all the work," says Coco. "We are delighted to have you in our home. Certainly, you are excused."

Chingas pales as he tries to rise.

"Please, let me help you to the mat," says Daniel. Chana and Amalie follow and cover their grandfather with quilts.

Before sunrise Chingas awakens, feeling invigorated and hungry. He lays in the dark until he sees a light descending the stairway.

"Chingas, are you awake?" asks Coco Wozniak.

"I am," he says, arising.

"Are you hungry?"

"Very."

"Come to the table. I have some leftovers from last night."

Chingas sits at the table. "What time is it?"

"It will be time to rise in about an hour. I knew you'd awaken early."

The stairs creak. "Good morning, Chingas. Feeling better?" asks Daniel.

"Yes," says Chingas. "Perhaps we can get out of your hair today."

"Not a chance," says Daniel. "This weather will have us socked in through today. Do you hear the wind? It will drift the snow, making passage impossible."

Chingas walks to the window, cups his hands around his face and peers out. "The snow is blowing sideways."

"These things usually blow themselves out in three days. It might be clear tomorrow," Daniel says.

Chingas hobbles back to the table. "Looking out there, I wonder how we would have survived if we hadn't found you." says Chingas. "I had planned to stay at the castle but that it was full of Red soldiers."

"The Red Army, here?" asks Daniel.

"Aye. At the castle. Probably pinned down from this storm."

"I'll get some of my men on it at first light," says Daniel.

"I saw last evening that you are a man of faith," says Chingas.

"Yes, we're Christians," says Daniel.

"We are Jews," says Chingas.

"The girls told us," says Daniel. "They said their mother is Christian."

"That she was."

"Was?"

"I'm not sure she lived through the last raid. We expected a raid within an hour of the time I got the children out of Kovno. Our family was the target of it, especially their mother, but I haven't mentioned my suspicions to the girls."

"Your villages could certainly use a Riflemen's Association," says Daniel. "The only way to stave off persecution is to be armed and be ready."

"We've been victims ever since they disarmed us," says Chingas. "They don't even spare the children. I thought we could take back our country with this new regime, but now we're even worse off."

"Chana and Amalie said they would board a freedom ship in Bremen," says Daniel.

"That's what we call it. I'm hoping to sell the mare and wagon when we get there and purchase tickets for them."

"You won't be going with them?"

"No. I need to find my grandson, Otto."

"You'll walk to Bremen then all the way back to Kovno?"

"Yes."

Daniel studies Chingas. "I don't doubt it, Chingas. When you come back through, stop here and stay with us. You'll always be welcome."

"Here's some food," says Coco. "Eat up, Chingas."

"Thank you," says Chingas. "Daniel, I don't want to hold hands with you, but would you pray that this food will help me get my strength back?"

THROUGHOUT THE DAY Amalie and Chana scrub corners, make candles, shovel the barn and cook. When Chingas tries to assist, Coco chases him back to his chair. He allows the women to wash his clothes and he wears blankets while they dry by the fire.

Just after sundown Daniel returns and hangs up his guns. "Something smells good," he says.

Dinner is another feast, and this time Chingas enjoys it. The women clear the dishes and Daniel spreads a map across the table.

"See here," he says to Chingas, pointing at the map, "this is your trek so far, Kovno through Zbaraz. The boys and I paid a visit to the Red Army today. You were right—they were holed up at the castle. They are part of the western front—a Russian assault. You and your granddaughters have been in the thick of their advance."

"No wonder we kept running into them," Chingas says.

"I found out what their plans are. They will be following the lowlands on the north side of Krakow, here. You and your granddaughters must follow the lowlands on the south side, through Prague. Then you can follow this route to Dresden and catch a river boat to Bremen. I marked it for you on this map."

"All right. The wind died down this afternoon. We'll be leaving in the morning."

"The snow drifts will be difficult until you drop down onto this southern route. There's quite a bit of activity through this part so it should be smooth all the way to Dresden." A drop of water falls onto the map and Daniel looks at Chingas.

"Sorry, Daniel," Chingas says, wiping his tears. "I was just remembering the prayer I uttered before I came to your home. I thought God didn't like me when the Red Army was in the castle and I was so spent. He brought us here, to safety. My strength is back. I will be able to get my granddaughters safely to Bremen, thanks to you and Coco."

"Thanks be to God," Daniel says.


BEFORE SUNUP, the Wozniak kitchen is alive with activity. Coco prepares stacks of food for the Meinrel's trek. Chingas dresses in his clean clothing and joins Daniel outside to help clear a pathway to the main road.

"The Red Army won't be in front of you on this road," says Daniel. "We've swept them away for now, but I expect more are on their way. You and your granddaughters should be able to stay ahead of them until the road turns south. After that, you'll be out of their path."

Chingas looks up, panting. "We've shoveled our way to the main road. I can get the wagon through if the girls push."

Daniel breathes hard and rises to catch his breath. "Did you see that blue rock on my step?"

"No, I didn't notice it," says Chingas.

Daniel motions for him to follow and walks back to the house. Chana, Amalie and Coco come out of the house with bundles of food.

Daniel points. "That's the blue rock. All the Riflemen keep one on their steps. You can stop at any of those homes and they will help you and your granddaughters. I've sent word up the line. Use my name."

"I will. Thank you."

Amalie and Chana stand on either side of Daniel and he puts his arms around them. "You three have a very tough journey ahead, and in the winter months no less. Just before you get into Germany you'll find a bridge that crosses a great divide. It's a railroad bridge and you never know when a train is coming.

Don't trust it. Follow the divide north until you get to the footbridge."

"How much time will that add?" asks Chingas.

"A good week—maybe more with the wagon."

"A week?" Chingas asks. "We must be in Bremen by the middle of December or we'll miss the last freedom ship."

"It's risky to cross that railroad bridge. Some people wait for the train and then cross, but I wouldn't—not with a wagon."

The Meinrels bid their hosts farewell and Daniel places hay into the back of their wagon. "For your mare, Chingas. We want her looking healthy when you sell her in Bremen."

Chingas pats the mare forward.


In the early evening of December 5, 1920, Chingas, Chana and Amalie reach the railroad bridge. The bridge has no side rails. It spans a deep chasm lined with rock cliffs and trees. Down the middle of the bridge runs the railroad track and on either side is about a half meter of wood.

"Germany is just across this bridge," says Chana.

"It's plenty wide for the wagon wheels, but I'm worried how the mare will step across the slats," says Chingas. "I wouldn't be able to rush her."

"It's a quarter mile or so across," says Amalie. "We're almost there, Grandfather."

"I think I hear a train," says Chana.

The three step away from the bridge and listen.

"That makes our choice simpler," says Chingas. "Daniel said that some people wait until a train clears and then they cross."

"What if another train comes while we're in the middle?" asks Amalie.

"We'll hear it," says Chana. "We don't have an extra week to find the foot bridge."

"Stop worrying about me, Chana. I'll be all right even if we decide to find the foot bridge," says Chingas. "Your concern for me mustn't affect your decision about crossing. My first priority is your safety."

"Here comes the train," says Amalie. It looks like we'll get about a five-minute warning. That's plenty of time for me and Chana to get a safe distance, but…" She doesn't finish.

"And you don't worry about me either, Amalie," Chingas says. "I'll make it across. I'll just be slower because of the mare and wagon."

The train rips loudly over the tracks, whistle blaring. The girls cover their ears.

"We need to make the decision right now," yells Chingas above the clickity-clacking. "There's only one fair way. The short straw means we take the shortest route. The long straw means we find the foot bridge. Either way, there's a big risk so we have to promise that we won't question the decision." Chana and Amalie nod in agreement. "Chana, you draw."

Chana picks a straw hidden inside Chingas's palms.

"You drew the short one," says Chingas. "We cross here. You two grab your satchels and get across the bridge as fast as you can."

Chana and Amalie grab their bags from the back of the wagon. The young women step across the bridge, preferring to hop on the middle ties than walk along the edge.

"Come on, old friend," says Chingas patting the horse. He aligns the wagon wheels to flank the railroad ties and allows the mare to find her footing on the slats. "Come on," he encourages.

The mare makes slow progress, meter by meter, finding solid steps.

"Come on, you can do it," yells Amalie. "You're halfway here."

Chingas clicks his tongue and the mare tugs, but the wagon doesn't budge. Chingas crawls under the wagon to find the hold-up. A broken rail caught the wooden wheel of the wagon. The mare continues to pull, burying the wheel into the steel.

"Whoa, girl," says Chingas. He tugs and pulls and heaves against the wheel, but it doesn't budge. He crawls back to the front of the wagon and holds onto the mare's reins.

"I need to try to back up the wagon," he yells to the young women. Chingas encourages the mare backwards. The wagon doesn't move.

"Yi yi yi, I'm going to lose this wagon" he mutters. He takes off his top hat, scratches his head and wipes his brow. He reaches into the wagon, grabs Otto's hat and shoves it into his sweater.

"I'll just loosen the mare and bring her across," he yells to his granddaughters.

"Grandfather, I hear a whistle," yells Amalie. "Grandfather, run! A train is coming."

Chingas unhitches the bridle with shaking hands and loosens the reins. The tracks under his feet vibrate and the whistle gets louder.

"The wagon is blocking our way back," he mutters. "You and I can't make it across before the train gets here." Chingas wipes his eyes and pats the mare's head.

"Grandfather, get off the bridge!" the girls are jumping and screaming.

"It's too late," he sobs, stepping to the edge of a tie.

The bridge pitches under his feet and the whistle blasts steady and shrill. The train hits the bridge at high speed. Chingas locks eyes with the engineer and falls off the bridge, hooking onto a tie with the reins. The bridge rumbles and shakes the reins loose and he grabs the tie, hides his face and hangs on.

The train hits the horse and wagon in a sickening explosion. Kindling and carnage fall around Chingas and into the ravine. The roar drowns his screams. He clings to the tie, pitching violently, refusing to let it shake him loose, but the shaking, rumbling and roaring continue on and on. Finally it ends, but the deafening sound continues inside Chingas's head. Chingas can't move. The lower part of his body dangles over the chasm and the upper half is frozen in place.

"Grandfather, Grandfather." He can hear their hysteria but he cannot speak.

"Pull, Amalie, pull." Chana's voice sounds like it's coming from a deep fog. He feels their small hands pull on his wrists, then his elbows. His body is stuck. Now their hands are on the waist of his pants. He knows the bottom half of his body is hanging over the edge of the bridge. He doesn't like them reaching over the edge like that, but the words won't come. His granddaughters' efforts win. His body moves to the top of the bridge. They turn him over. He looks at them but they seem far away. They roll him to the center of the bridge and each takes a leg. The railroad ties bump his head and rub his backside as they drag him across the bridge to Germany. His arms rise above his head, limp and useless. They roll him off the road into a snow ditch.

"We need to keep him warm," says Chana. "Get our travel dresses from our satchels and cover him. Come, we'll lay next to him."

An hour later Chingas sits up and weeps. His granddaughters pull him to his feet and support his steps.

"We must find shelter," says Amalie. "I see lights ahead. Maybe there's a blue rock on the porch."

"Probably not in Germany," says Chana. "Maybe they will allow us to stay in their barn."

And they did.

# CHAPTER 17
## December 1920

Amalie inspects Chana's buttons then helps her brush away a crease from the skirt of her best dress, then Chana holds up the blanket so Amalie can change in privacy. They are in a quiet alley only a few meters from the busy port in Bremen, Germany, and are using it as a changing facility. Chingas had been uncertain he could make it to this seaport with his two granddaughters, but the three had survived almost four months of cruel weather, trekking across three countries. All three of them resemble skeletons, but with the natural beauty and graces the girls possess, people along the way were drawn to them, and they received assistance in their neediest hours.

Chingas agonizes over all of his failings since leaving Kovno with his three grandchildren. The trek was worse than he had ever imagined. The first week, he lost his precious Otto to the marauding Red Army. For days after, they had walked in numbing silence, often crying. At night they sometimes slept under the wagon, even after the snow came. The faithful old mare had pulled the wagon over many rivers and streams, allowing them to stay dry. After the horse was killed, his granddaughters had not understood why he cried so mournfully. They had kept reminding him of all the trials he had stoically endured, thinking it would somehow help him in his weakness.

He could not tell them that without the old mare they had nothing to sell in Bremen to pay for their passage.

Now, at the end of their 2,500-kilometer journey, the S.S. Sierra Nevada, an American ship, is listing in the harbor, and the girls are convinced it is waiting for them.

"Chana, Amalie. Listen to your bony old grandfather. There is no money to purchase your passage to America, but I will work and, perhaps in a few months, God willing, there will be another ship."

The girls stop their preparations and stare at him, giggle, and turn and look past the building and point to the top masts of their ship.

"It's our ship, Grandfather. It waited for us," says Amalie.

They chatter and giggle and Chingas throws his hands up, feeling old to his core. His resilient granddaughters are alive with anticipation. He bows his head and considers praying. Surely the God that made the earth and parted the seas can help his granddaughters board a vessel. Perhaps it isn't too much to ask. He closes his eye and furrows his brows. He takes a breath, expels it, and opens his eye.

"I have no words. What can I ask more? We are here, in Germany, a great miracle and an answer to Galayna's prayer. How can I ask and ask without giving anything back?" He feels a tap on his shoulder and turns to see Amalie. Her dark hair is pulled to one side and falls in natural curls, and she is placing a hat carefully on her head at a slight angle. Chana reaches over and corrects the angle. Chana's hair is exactly the same, but pulled back on the opposite side. He looks from one granddaughter to the other. Amalie's eyes dance, while Chana's are soft.

"How do we look?" asks Amalie.

"Breathtaking," decrees her grandfather, his aged feelings evaporating. "Sparkling, youthful, extraordinary." He kisses them.

"Come, grandfather," says Amalie, tugging on his arm.

"No, no, no. Wait, wait, wait. My granddaughters, please listen. We have no money for your passage. All we have is our faith, and I have mighty little of that. Now, if your grandmother were here, she would be able to get you aboard that ship with her faith, but all three of us know, I just don't have enough."

"Grandfather," Chana scolds. "Of course you have enough faith. Look, around. We are in Bremen! We made it! Grandmother's prayers are with us. And your prayers too. I've heard you praying."

"Praying, yes, but believing, no. I learned a long time ago, God only listens to women."

The girls giggle and walk to either side of their grandfather, each tucking an arm into his. With their resilient energy throbbing into his sides, Chingas is transformed from a patch-eyed, hobbling old man to a gallant escort of two graceful young women.

"You are right, Chana. We've made it all the way to Bremen. Unfortunately, we used up all our miracles getting here. This might be our journey's end for a while. It would take a mighty big miracle to get aboard that ship, as penniless as we are. I'm too inadequate to ask God again."

They enter the harbor office and the girls stand by the door, encouraging their grandfather forward. Chingas respectfully removes his hat and approaches the harbormaster to request passage for two to New York, but feeling the impossibility of the petition even before it escapes his lips.

"Sir," he implores apologetically, "I have two passengers who need to secure passage aboard the S.S. Sierra Nevada."

The harbormaster does not look up as he replies. "Sorry, nothing left. Completely sold out."

Chingas's brows arch. He stumbles backward, the air sucked from his lungs and the room darkening. The girls rush to his sides.

"Grandfather, you're pale and weaving. What's wrong?" asks Amalie. "It will be all right, Grandfather. That ship has been waiting for us. It will not depart without us. I know it."

Chingas regains his stance. Amalie's face, intent and radiant, encourages him, but he has no power to help her. Chingas pats her hand.

"Amalie, you and Chana are the unfortunate victims of my lacking spirit, as decrepit and worn as my body." Chingas looks back at the ticket counter. "I'll try again if you and Chana will pray with as much faith as your grandmother. That is the only way such a miracle can happen."

"All right, Grandfather. We'll pray. You go talk with the agent," Chana says. The girls bow their heads. Chingas walks back to the ticket counter.


The harbormaster grumbles under his breath. "Blast the labor party for sending all my underlings to work in the camps. Now I have to sell boat tickets to the likes of..."

"I must have passage for two," demands Chingas pounding his fist on the counter.

The harbormaster looks at the thin and tattered old man with his crooked eyepatch. "Sorry," he snaps. "All that's left is one bunk in steerage. Or, of course, one cabin in first class," he sneers. He resumes muttering to himself.

A young woman steps in front of the bedraggled patriarch. Her dark, soft eyes beguile him and he notices her smooth, clean hair and refined, delicate features.

"My sister and I will take the one bed in steerage," says Chana. "We'll sleep together."

"My, my. You are a blessing in this ugly world," says the ticketer. "I doubt that two could share one of those small bunks, but it's not my business if you want to try. I won't charge you for two beds, but I will have to include the other costs of food, landing expenses and transportation."

"That's fine, sir," says Chana, pulling Amalie beside her. "How much is the passage for my sister and me?"

"Two of you! Beauties like you do not belong in the foul-smelling steerage area. Are you certain you would not be more comfortable in the cabin? I think I can arrange it for almost the same price," he offers, smiling. "I must be feeling generous today."

"Please, sir, how much for the steerage?" insists Chana.

"Steerage for two people, less one bed, will be 51.50."

"I…I've never even seen that much money," says Chana. She looks at Chingas, her eyes searching and confused.

Amalie pokes Chana with her elbow. "Chana, do you see those shiphands preparing the ship? We don't have much time." Amalie steps to the ticket counter.

"My sister and I must be on that ship," she says. She removes her only possession from her pocket – the broach her mother gave her the day she fled Kovno. "Sir, I have a precious broach, which I hope you will accept for the required passage." She opens her hand and gingerly extends the broach to the harbormaster. Amalie bites her lip as the harbormaster takes the broach. He fingers it respectfully,

"I've seen much better," he says, holding the broach under his lamp. He looks at Amalie's face, and shrugs his shoulders. "I think this is adequate for the cabin." He writes paperwork and pushes a document to the young women. Chingas steps between them and picks it up with reverence and holds it to his chest. The patch-eyed man's face contorts and his chin quivers involuntarily. The harbormaster stares at the old man. "Am I witnessing the end or beginning of a saga?" he asks.

"Why have you helped us?" asks Chingas.

The harbormaster raises his eyebrows. "Your broach, such as it is, has purchased two young women first-class passage to America. Why question a gift? That door will lead you to the ramp. The Sierra Nevada has been anchored here for a month awaiting the tide. You two will be the last passengers."

Amalie and Chana pick up their small bundle, and links arms with their grandfather, leading him to the door. The three emerge into the chilly morning and stroll to the ship where a few sailors concentrate on ropes and rising waters.

"Chana, take Otto's hat." Chingas pulls the hat from his shirt and holds it in both of his hands. Someday, God willing, you can return it to him."

Chana wraps her hands around her grandfather's and takes the hat. "I will, grandfather."

"You two go ahead and board the ship. It may be a few days before they pull up the anchor, but I would like you to get settled and have a place to sleep tonight."

"Where will you go?" asks Amalie.

"To find Otto." Chingas kisses his granddaughters.

"I love you, Grandfather," Chana murmurs, nestling into his whiskers and kissing him.

"I love you, Grandfather," whispers Amalie, laying her head against his chest.

He holds their faces, kisses them, pulls them close with his powerful arms and holds them.

"You are my most prized possessions," he says. "Please God, watch over my precious granddaughters."

He walks them to the bottom of the gangplank, and when they try to turn again to him, he physically prevents it, pushing them onto the plank and waving off resistance. When they step aboard and show their paperwork to an official, Chingas watches the man point to a direction on the ship. Chingas turns and limps away.

Chingas makes his way around a building and into an alleyway. He leans his back against cold bricks and raises his face to heaven. His shoulders shake and his throat swells. Sobs break past quivering lips and jump in visible puffs into the brisk air. His back slides downward until he crouches on the ground. When he composes himself he walks from the alleyway's seclusion back to the docks, but the ship is gone. During his crying time, the ships bells sounded, the ropes were loosed, coal was shoveled into the fire of her belly, and the S.S. Sierra Nevada headed for deep water.

Chingas turns and takes his first haltered step toward Kovno.

# CHAPTER 18

## *December 1920 through January 1921*

Amalie stares at the ceiling of the old ship's grand suite, Chana beside her.

"I didn't know my eyes had so many tears," she says.

Chana sniffs. "Did you see it in his eyes?"

"Aye. He has determined to find our little brother," says Amalie.

Chana sits up, wipes her wet face on her sleeve and walks to the portal window. "We've been reminiscing far too long. We should figure out where we are and where we're going."

"I can't let go yet," Amalie whimpers. "If we stop talking about them we may never get them back."

Chana walks around the bed and sits beside her sister. "Mother would tell us to get up and figure things out. You remember how brave she was."

"I know," says Amalie, wiping her nose and sitting up. She buries her face in her skirt and bawls.

Chana puts her arm around Amalie. "That's enough. Let's wash our traveling clothes. We'll probably be on this ship for a couple weeks."

Amalie dries her face and looks around. "You're right. Mother would scold me for acting like this. I must be stronger."

Chana opens the door by the closet. "Look! It's a privacy."

Amalie squeezes in beside her and bends down to look at a large porcelain square. "I think it's for bathing."

"It's huge, stuck right on the floor. Are those spickets? Why does it have two spickets?" Chana turns the knobs. "One is hot water, and the water just disappears down that hole."

"Baths!" says Amalie, pulling at her buttons.

"Not until we get our travel clothing washed," says Chana

"But if we bathe first we can wash our clothes in our bath water."

Chana plugs the hole and turns on the water. "Good idea."

Amalie picks up a small round puff. "Mmm, Chana smell. I think its soap."

Chana leans over to sniff and the puff falls into the water. "Look at the bubbles!" she laughs.

After bathing they wrap themselves in the soft bathrobes hanging behind the door, and dip their traveling clothes into the soapy water.

"They should soak for awhile," says Chana.

"Sit here and let me brush your hair," says Amalie. Chana sits and Amalie starts the long process of detangling while resuming their conversation. "And then we'll get off the ship in America," Amalie says.

"But then what?" asks Chana. "What will we do when we get to America?"

"Maybe I can find a job in a dress shop," says Amalie. "I can sew just about anything."

"We don't know the language, or the customs," says Chana.

Amalie blows softly through her lips. "It's a busy city. We couldn't sleep in the open without a proper escort."

Chana closes her eyes. "We must figure this out before we get there. How long do we have?"

"A couple weeks, I think," says Amalie.

"I'm the eldest, but I don't know what I should do. Oh, mother, what would you have me do?"

"She would want you to find us a proper escort," says Amalie.

"That would be our father or grandfather, and neither one will be with us," says Chana.

"They aren't the only proper escorts for young women," says Amalie stepping around to look into Chana's face. "A husband would also be a proper escort."

Chana's eyebrows arch and her jaw drops. "A husband! For me?"

Amalie swallows, moisture filling up her lower lids. She nods. "We must find a husband for you Chana. You were almost betrothed once. Remember?"

"Toppur."

"Yes, Toppur. Do you wonder about him?"

"Sometimes. We never had a chance to know one another before—before that Purim raid. He was good, but I wasn't convinced we were a match."

Amalie resumes brushing.

"You're right, Amalie. If I had a good husband we would be cared for."

"How will we ever find a match?" Amalie asks. "We don't have a shadchan—a matchmaker!"

Chana stands up and Amalie sits so Chana can brush her hair. Amalie's eyes fixate on the wall light as Chana brushes.

"I'm not sure a matchmaker would help," says Chana. "A shadchan matches people who have similar backgrounds and beliefs. I'm sure we won't find a Russian Jewish peasant, and even if we do, I don't think he would have the means to help us in America. How will I find a good husband? We can't walk around, looking at the men."

"What would mother tell you to do?" asks Amalie.

"Pray."

Amalie stops Chana's brush. "Then we must pray, with all our hearts."

They drop to their knees, bow their heads, cover their eyes with their fingertips and move their lips. A few minutes later Amalie sits back on her haunches and waits for Chana to finish.

"Amen." Chana frowns. "I prayed for a match, and then I prayed for a good shadchan."

"A good shadchan would be expected to have a critical eye and great insight," says Amalie, raising an eyebrow.

"But even if we found such a matchmaker, we have no money to pay her."

Amalie stands up and pulls Chana to her feet. "Perhaps you already have a good shadchan and just don't know it." She places her hand on her heart. "I feel the gift of the shadchan coming on me."

"Amalie, you have no experience. What if you found an inappropriate match?"

"I have a little experience. I listened to the questions of Rabbi Wecht's matchmaker. It's more important that your outlooks are similar than your past. I will ask excellent questions."

"What questions?"

"A good match must care for both of us when we get to America. He must have a home for us and for our family when they come from Russia."

"You do sound wise, little sister. Perhaps God gave you the gift while we were praying."

Amalie squeezes Chana's curls. "It's important that you find favor in your husband's eyes."

"Yes, I must," Chana says. "Did you notice anyone that might be a match?"

Amalie frowns. "Maybe. Remember the young officer at the top of the ramp?"

"The one who asked to help us?"

Amalie tilts her head. "And you told him no."

"Well of course I refused his help. He seemed so important for such a young officer. I didn't think we needed him to leave his position to carry our two small satchels."

Amalie tilts her head and runs her finger across Chana's furled brow. "And did you hear him speak?"

"He spoke formal German. When I didn't answer him right away he asked me again in Russian."

"That is a sign," says Amalie.

"It is?"

"Yes. He asked you twice, so when he asks a third time you will be free to accept."

"Amalie, feel my heart—it's beating so rapidly, telling me it is right that you are my shadchan."

Amalie touches Chana's chest. "Your heart is right."

Chana jumps at the loud rapping at the door and, opens it to see a freckle-faced ship-boy holding a large fruit basket. Amalie moves in front of Chana.

"Good evening," says the ship-boy. "This is from Chief Jarmon. May I set it on your table?"

Amalie steps aside and allows him to enter.

"Chief Jarmon invites you to join him at the captain's table for dinner this evening."

"I-I-W-We can't," says Chana.

Amalie moves Chana aside. "What my sister means is that we just washed our dresses, and we have no dry clothing."

"Let me take your dresses to the laundry," says the boy. "I'll have them pressed dry and bring them right back."

Amalie retrieves the dripping clothing. "These two dresses take a long time to press."

"Don't worry," says the boy. "Our laundry workers are very good. They will get them done."

"Thank you," says Chana.

"Is Chief Jarmon the officer that met us at the top of the ramp?" asks Amalie.

"Yes, he is," says the boy, holding the dripping clothing outside the doorway and backing up. "His name is Layland Jarmon."

"Layland Jarmon," says Chana. "Chief Layland Jarmon."

"Can you get the door behind me?" the boy asks.

Amalie closes the door and bites her lips together. "I think God heard our prayers."

"Layland Jarmon," Chana says. "He had a polite demeanor. I'd like to see him again, Amalie. I wonder if it's all right to walk around the ship."

"I think you should wear your hair in side ringlets," says Amalie. "Sit here and let me get started."

An hour later the ship-boy returns with the pressed and starched dresses and Amalie inspects the detailed care someone took with the iron.

"Your coats won't be ready until tomorrow," he says. "I brought you these shawls to keep the evening chill away."

"No, please," Amalie says. "We'll be fine."

"Chief Jarmon would like to take you for a stroll before dinner. Could he come by at four bells—a half hour from now?"

"That should be fine," says Amalie, closing the door.

Amalie slips into her work dress and Chana steps into her starched Sabbath dress.

"Wear my slip too," says Amalie. "It will add body to the skirt." She helps Chana with her buttons, sash and ribbons and pinches her cheeks when the knock comes at the door.

Amalie opens it, standing a little behind, allowing her sister to fully view this prospective pursuer.

Layland Jarmon, twenty-five, is a full hand taller than Grandmother. He removes his hat to reveal thick brown hair, which he wears straight back. His demeanor appears confident, but Amalie sees an edge of nervousness in his hazel eyes. Creases from weather-exposure run across the forehead of his tanned face. She can see his heavily-muscled frame even through his dress blues.

"Miss Chana Meinrel?" he asks.

"Yes, Chief Layland Jarmon."

"Just Layland."

"Layland."

Amalie sees moisture gathering around Chana's eyes. "I am Amalie Meinrel, Chana's sister and matchmaker," she says.

"Aha," he says. "Would you like to go for a stroll? I'd like to show you around the ship."

"You speak better German than we do," says Chana, taking his arm. "We come from a small Jewish village in Russia."

He smiles at her and holds the door for them. "That explains the dialect. "This way, Miss Chana and Miss Amalie." The two sisters follow Layland to the main deck. A healthy breeze fills the sails.

"Matchmakers serve an important purpose in many countries, Miss Amalie. You're the youngest matchmaker I've ever met."

"This is my first match," says Amalie.

"Are you thinking that I might be a match for Chana?"

"Maybe, maybe not," says Amalie.

"I only have a few minutes to show you the ship. I'd like you to feel comfortable walking around." He offers an arm to each of them. Chana links herself to his arm but Amalie walks to the far side of Chana and links arms with her sister.

Layland shows them the galley, the lounge and the bridge, introducing them to personnel. He points to other areas they could explore on their own and takes them back to their cabin. "I have some duties to attend to prior to dinner. My ship-boy will call for you."

Chana looks up at him and smiles. "Thank you, Layland."

Layland's eyes don't pull away from Chana's until Amalie steps between them and closes the door.

"I hope Layland Jarmon is a match," Chana says.

"Aye," says Amalie. "I must prove him."

Layland climbs the steps to the captain's bridge. "Captain Kent," he says. "I talked with Dom and he'll hold the engines at full until this trough moves out."

Captain Kent motions and Layland follows him to the after deck. The captain offers Layland a cigar and they light up.

"How long have we been sailing these seas together?" asks Captain Kent.

"Eight years, sir—ever since I left law school and came back to sea."

"Counting those youthful years when you were shanghaied, you've been a sailor for about thirteen years," says Captain Kent. "I still credit you for saving our ship in the North Sea when we had to cross that mine field."

"Yes, sir," says Layland. "It was tricky. I had to feel my way through."

The captain puffs on his cigar. "In all our years together, I've never seen you take to a woman before today."

"I've never been drawn to a woman before now," says Layland. "When I saw Chana coming out of the shore shack, I couldn't take my eyes off her. I feel so, so—"

"Happy?" asks the captain.

"Yes," says Layland. "And nervous. Her sister is her matchmaker, and I fear I won't stack up."

The captain chuckles. "Only a woman can make a man like you nervous." He takes another draw from his cigar. "Approach it like you did that mine field—you moved us forward inch by inch. Other ships weren't so lucky. You have to put your mind to it, boy."

"I wish we had more time," says Layland. "We'll be in New York in a couple weeks and I can't lose her."

"Do you know how to delegate?"

"No, sir."

"If you're going to be captain someday you may as well learn," says the captain. "Get Eddie to take your engine runs, and ask the bosun to cover the ropes. That should save you extra hours each day."

"Thank you, Captain Kent. I'll do that."

"Don't botch it, boy—inch by inch."


TWO WEEKS LATER, Layland opens his eyes and looks at the clock. 05:00. He jumps out of bed, showers, lathers his chin and sharpens his razor. He looks in the mirror and points his razor at his reflection. "Today counts," he says. "Don't botch it." He tilts his head, takes a swipe with the razor, and swishes the blade in the pan of water to rid the soap. Conversations and magical moments with Chana replay inside his brain.

Meeting Chana in Bremen was unexpected. It had been flattering to imagine such an enchanting woman willing to consider him husband material, and he hopes each one of his answers will be met with Amalie's pronouncement, Tov. He can't imagine his life without Chana in it.

During the four days the ship docked in Liverpool Amalie and Chana learned more about him than anyone had ever known. Amalie was even able to get the details of his childhood experiences at sea which he hadn't even shared with his father.

He considers how it makes him feel when they meet to walk the deck and she slips her hand into the bend of his elbow and smiles up at him, Amalie on the other side of Chana, always interrogating. He sees his expression in the mirror. "Goony bird," he chides himself. "Focus!"

In spite of their delicate appearance Chana and Amalie are physically strong. They had sea sickness the second and third days, which they ignored, leaning over the railing and chumming the water as necessary. Chana was especially solicitous to other ill passengers and helped set a young boy's leg. During a storm of sleet, he found the two Russian sisters strolling the deck as usual while other passengers hunkered inside their cabins.

Yesterday Chana had taken his arm and pressed closer to him. He could feel her warmth and the rise and fall of her breathing against his arm. He had studied her features as she gazed down at the deck, her long black lashes resting against her white and rosy skin, and her hair ringlets jiggling with each step. He would do anything to hold her in his arms. Amalie had interrupted his thoughts.

"Are you circumcised?" Amalie had asked.

"No," he answered.

"Why not?"

"My parents were Catholic. The Catholic church didn't require that I be circumcised."

"Our mother was Orthodox," Chana had said.

They walked in silence a few paces before Amalie had asked, "Will you have your children circumcised?"

Layland had answered "Not my daughters."

Chana squeezed his arm and pressed her face into his sleeve, giggling. He had impressed her! Amalie, on the other hand, was deadpan, and Amalie's decision held his fate, so he apologized. "I'm sorry, Amalie. I was flip. To me religion is highly personal. If Chana desires that our sons be circumcised I will not object."

"What will you teach your children about God?" Amalie asked.

"My family baptized me Catholic and Chana is part Jewish and part Orthodox. Chana and I haven't practiced the religion of our births, but I believe we should settle on a religion that suits our family."

He had thought he answered well until Amalie asked, "Why?"

Inch-by-inch, he told himself before he answered. "God designed the family so a child has both a mother and a father. Together, parents teach their child to pray and have faith, to help the child when they're not around. When a child is grown, they will either accept their parents' opinions of divinity or create their own opinions—they choose for themselves at that point, but when they're small, parents would be wrong not to give their children a basis in faith."

They walked along quietly until Amalie finally said, "Tov."

Today Amalie will allow Chana to walk alone with him, and the thought both excites and weakens him. Tonight he will talk with Amalie about what she calls "the ketubah," and whatever that is, he will agree. His only need is to be Chana's husband.

At 10:00 Layland knocks at the door of the suite and Chana answers. "I know our date isn't until 11:00, but I couldn't wait," he says.

Chana smiles. "I'm ready."

Amalie sits on the bed, writing.

"Are you writing the Ketubah?" Layland asks.

"Yes," says Amalie. "It will be ready when you return."

Chana takes Layland's hand and he leads her to the deck, which is littered with belongings of passengers. Layland motions to a seaman and points to the debris. The seaman calls for subordinates and they police the area. For several minutes Chana and Layland walk, quiet and close. Chana leans her head against his arm

"Chana, you haven't asked me anything. Surely there are questions you want answered."

Chana stops and moves away from him. "I'm not sure how to ask my question," she says.

Layland studies her nervousness. "It's okay, Chana. You can ask me anything."

"Have I found favor in your eyes?" she asks.

"Yes, of course," he says. "I want to marry you, Chana. I can't imagine my life without you. What's bothering you, sweetheart? You're trembling."

"I am the eldest so I must do the right thing."

"I hope the right thing would be to marry me," says Layland.

"But you are a man of the sea."

"Yes."

"Amalie and I, we don't have any place to live. You live at sea but I...I don't know where we will live." Chana wipes her eyes.

"Oh, Chana, sweetheart." He takes her hands. "You mustn't worry about that. You'll stay at my home in Chicago when I'm at sea."

"You have a home?" Chana asks.

"It isn't my home, but it's my grandmother's home—my mother's mother—Grandmother Abbott."

"She will allow us to live with her while you are at sea?" Chana asks.

"Of course. My Uncle Herschel also lives there and he will be thrilled to meet you. Please, Chana, please marry me—tomorrow, as soon as we're in the New York harbor. Captain Kent will marry us. When we disembark, you and Amalie will come to Chicago with me. You'll be comfortable and safe. I promise. Will you please marry me?"

Chana sobs, coughs, wipes her face, and looks into his eyes. "Yes, Layland. Yes, I will marry you."

He draws her in and feels her small frame fit perfectly against his. He kisses her, and kisses her again.

At four bells the next morning passengers and crew members assemble in foggy dampness to witness Captain Kent perform a short marriage ceremony on deck, establishing a life-long union between Chana Meinrel and Layland Gaylord Jarmon.

# CHAPTER 19

## *January 1921*

Layland checks his pocket-watch. "11:50. We're coming into Chicago right on time."

Amalie presses her cheek against the window of the train, straining to see ahead. "Chicago is a very big city," says Amalie.

"Two and a half million people," says Layland.

"Two and a half million and two," says Amalie.

"The train is very fast," says Chana.

"We traveled eight hundred miles in just twenty-one hours," says Layland. "It's the Twentieth Century Limited. There will be a faster train in a few months." He stands and opens the above-seat storage. "Better wrap up. It looks like freezing sleet out there. I hope you can tolerate Chicago's harsh weather."

Chana smiles. "We can."

Layland descends the steps first and turns to help Chana. He keeps them close as they jostle through the railyard and through the busy station, and he listens to their chatter about the way Chicago women dress.

"That one," says Amalie. "It shows a little ankle. Don't worry. I can needle it."

"Look at their shoes," says Chana. "They wear heels."

"Neither one of you should fret," says Layland. "This is the shopping cspital of America, and the four top deisgners live here. Come on. We'll take that cab."

Within a few minutes the cab stops in front of a three-story gray-stone Victorian, with steeply pitched, irregular-shaped roof and dominant front gable. A dramatic second-level terrace forms a shelter over the large front porch.

"Welcome to your new home," Layland says, guiding the gawking sisters up the front steps. He unlocks the heavy wood door and pulls Chana to him. "It is an American custom for a husband to carry his bride across the threshold of their first home." He lifts Chana into his arms, steps into the house, sets her down, and turns to invite Amalie inside.

"Layland! Is that you?" A striking woman with painted features and short, wavy gray hair, walks down the stairs holding the gold railing. A dark gray satin skirt and white blouse trimmed in rows of soft lace grace her posture-perfect tall frame. She walks into Layland's arms and kisses him. "I was expecting you a few days ago! What have you brought me this time?" She notices Chana and Amalie and her smile disappears. "Lay! What is this?"

"Grandmother," Layland says. "I would like you to meet my wife, Chana Jarmon, and her younger sister, Amalie." Layland beckons toward the young women and, although they do not speak English, they realize they have just been introduced, and they curtsy, smiling at their new relative.

Grandmother Abbott grabs her chest, raises her brows and drops her chin. Her gaze follows Chana, head to toe.

"My new grandmother," Chana says in Russian, and steps forward to bestow a kiss, but the older woman bats her away.

"Wife!" Grandmother Abbott shrieks. "You mean you married this, this...?"

"Yes, Grandmother. Last week, aboard ship."

"And the other one?" she asks flicking a finger in Amalie's direction.

153

"This is Amalie Meinrel, Chana's younger sister. She and Chana must stay here when I go back out to sea. Please Grandmother, make them welcome."

His grandmother presses her lips together in a thin, hard line and squints her eyes. "I have a headache, Layland. Show them to the guest area if they must stay here." She turns on her heel and walks from the room. As she exits she calls over her shoulder, "Herschel will be home at six, and Harriet will serve dinner promptly at 6:30. See that your guests are apprised. And properly dressed for dinner."

"Really, Grandmother, I had hoped for a little civility," Layland calls after her. "How am I supposed to explain away your actions?"

Mother Abbott ignores him and continues up the stairs. Layland turns to Chana, her face pale and her eyes round and moist.

"Grandmother does not like us," says Chana.

"Don't worry, sweetheart," says Layland, taking her trembling body into his arms. She just has to know you to love you."

Layland shows Amalie to the guest room and escorts Chana to the room they will share.

"It's a wonderful room, my husband," Chana says. She walks to the bureau, full of Layland's travel memorabilia, and gives each item to Layland until the top is cleared. "Quite a bit larger than our whole house in Kovno I think." She gets Otto's hat from her bag and sets it in the middle of the bureau.

Layland dumps his memorbelia into a bottom drawer. "I think it is much too large," he teases, pulling her close. "We only need this much room." She giggles.

At 6:30 Layland escorts Chana and Amalie to the dinner table. They stand behind their chairs, waiting. When Herschel Abbott finally enters he flashes a smile at Chana and Amalie. "Layland, my brilliant nephew," he praises. "How did you ever do something so splendid?" He walks to Layland, places his arm around his shoulders and gazes at the two women.

Herschel is three years Layland's senior, but his balding head makes him appear older than thirty. They have been best friends since early childhood, but Herschel flaunts his title of "uncle."

"Herschel, I'd like you to meet my wife, Chana."

Herschel takes Chana's white hands and kisses them. "Welcome to our family, dearest Chana," Herschel bows.

Layland interprets for Chana and she smiles, bends and plants kisses on Herschel's hands.

"Oh, my!" says Herschel.

"And this is Amalie, Chana's sister," says Layland.

"Oh, my! What a magnificent creature." Herschel kisses Amalie's hands, and she stoops and kisses his. Herschel laughs.

Amalie leans to Chana. "We'll be all right when Layland leaves. Uncle Herschel is kind."


Over the next two days Chana and Amalie try to help with the washing, housework and cooking and get into trouble with their new grandmother. Herschel enrolls them in English classes, which steals the first hours of their mornings.

After the second day of classes Layland meets them after school.

"I'm taking you dress shopping," he says.

Amalie and Chana look at each other and raise their brows.

"Grandmother insists that you dress differently for dinner. I love your Russian Sabbath dresses, but Grandmother has other ideas. We may as well try to please her."

"Perhaps one dress—like we saw at the train station—with the dropped waist," says Amalie. "The designs were so different I need a closer look. I want to make our dresses. May we stop at a fabric store?"

"Of course, but after we go to McCarthy's—it's where Grandmother buys her dresses. She says they carry clothing from top designers."

Chana takes Layland's hand. "I'd like some shoes with heels."

Layland smiles. "I know just where to take you."

Inside McCarthy's dress shop, an overly-painted middle-aged woman with a cropped hairline, short skirt and fake French accent greets Layland and snubs Chana and Amalie. Layland explains the purpose of the visit.

"Si, of course, Misseur Abbott. I am Estella."

"My name's Jarmon, not Abbott," says Layland.

Estella rings a bell and two women come from the back, equally painted but younger. "Zees eees Madmoiselle Abbott's grrrrandson," Estelle says, rolling the 'r' as she points to Layland. "Bring zee Chanel and Suoers collections. Come, come ze leetle foreign ladies, you vill try on ze gowns, si?" The two younger saleswomen hold back the heavy drapery and Estelle guides Chana and Amalie into a mirrored room. "Come come, gentleman Abbott. Seeet, seeet."

Layland bends to Chana's ear. "I can't believe Grandmother likes this moron."

"Look, Chana!" Amalie runs to a manaquin draped with a solid brown satin gown. "It's cut on the bias. See the threads? The lines are so fluid."

"I like sleeves," says Chana. "None of these dresses have sleeves."

"Bring my wife a dress with sleeves," says Layland.

"Na na na na, Monsieur, ze sleeves for old ladies. Sleeves are not for this bella. Let me see, ah, yes, I mean, si, La blue and la grrreen Chanel. Move the screen, move the screen."

The two younger saleswomen move the heavy wood screen in front of Amalie and Chana to block Layland's view.

Layland listens to rustling and whispers until Estelle claps loudly and the two women move the screen. He sees Amalie first, in the green Chanel, and then Chana in the blue. Both are bare-footed. The sleeveless dresses show not only their ankles but much of the calves, all of their arms, more than enough of their breasts. Each dress has a non-existent waistline and belted hips, which doesn't make sense to Layland. He doesn't realize his mouth is open.

"La décolletage—very nice," says Estelle. "Maybe try another?"

Chana and Amalie look at each other and giggle, and Layland bursts out laughing. "No, Estelle, not another."

"Ah, si, I got it right the first time, but of course," Estelle grins, claps and the saleswomen lug the screen. Chana and Amalie change back into their dresses and Estelle takes the two Chanel dresses to the counter.

"I have ze ticket for ze two Chanel dresses," says Estelle.

"Keep it—not interested," says Layland, escorting the sisters out the door. He turns as he leaves and says, "At least learn to say 'yes' in French, Estelle. It's 'oui' not 'si.'"

Chana puts her arm into Layland's. "Thank you for not buying that dress," she says. "It was awful."

"But the other one would have been beautiful," says Amalie. "I need fabric to make our dresses."

"We can stop by the fabric store on the way to the shoe store," says Layland. "Do you mind if we walk a bit?"

"We know how to walk," says Chana.

Amalie gasps as they enter the fabric store. She walks down the rows, running her fingers over textures, sometimes stopping to feel a selvage and gaze at colors. "This one," she finally says.

Layland motions to a salesman. "We want this," he says.

"The chiffon?" asks the salesman. "What color, sir? We have it in blue, green, mauve and purple, as well as a few subtle patterns."

"All of them," says Layland.

"How many yards?" he asks.

"Enough of each to make two gowns," Layland says. "And some of that white that she's looking at."

"The satin?"

"Yes. Measure it out like the others."

"And matching thread?" asks the salesman.

"Yes. And ribbon."

Amalie picks out three needles and a ball of fine crochet thread and gives them to the clerk to include in the purchase. "Grandmother Abbott must tolerate our Sabbath dresses a little longer," she says.


Amalie spends every spare minute working tiny stitches into the purple chiffon. Two days before Layland leaves Chana tries it on.

"Amalie, it's a beautiful dress," says Chana. "Much nicer than any I saw at McCarthy's. I love the way you made the skirt." She twirls and the tear-shaped inserts in the skirt flow out from her hips in a profusion of movement. "This is the right style, with the dropped waist, but how did you get it to follow my body? The sleeves fit my arms perfectly, yet I can easily move my elbows."

"It's the bias cut," says Amalie. "It's like magic trick. It will make all our dresses fit nicely."

"All our dresses?"

"Layland purchased a lot of fabric, and I love to sew."

"And now I have a new dress. But you don't. How will you get your dress finished before Layland leaves? It took you days to finish this. I won't wear my dress unless you have a new dress too."

"I'll make a simpler one for me—like the one I saw on that maniquin at McCarthy's. If I start right now I should be able to finish it by tomorrow night. What color should my dress be?"

"Make it from the deep green," says Chana.


Early, on the morning of Layland's departure, Chana slips out of bed and hurries to Amalie's room. "Layland loves the way you did my hair when we strolled on the deck of the U.S.S. Sierra Nevada," she says.

"It will take at least an hour," says Amalie. "We barely have enough time. Sit here."

"How will you fix your hair?" asks Chana.

"I'll just twist these long braids on top of my head. Don't worry. It's you that must be remembered."

"Did you finish hemming your green dress?" asks Chana.

"It's all done, although I haven't tried it on yet."

Amalies catches Chana's black hair high, letting it fall into a spiral cascade from the top of her head to the middle of her back, and weaves purple and white ribbons through the curls.

"Yes, that's the way he likes it," she says, looking in a mirror.

"Here's your silk stockings," Amalie says.

Chana folds and gently pulls the stockings up her legs and attaches them to garters. Amalie helps her slide into her dress, and checks the edges of her hair to assure perfection.

"You finally get to wear your heels," says Amalie. Chana steps into her black heels with tiny heart shapes cut out of the rounded toes.

"I'll go downstairs and wait for Layland in the entry hall. You hurry and get ready," Chana says.

Amalie hugs her sister. "He won't forget you, Chana. No one could."

"I love him so much. I hope you're right." Chana flicks away a tear and hurries downstairs. Within a few minutes she hears Layland's steps.

"Oh, Chana!" he says, setting down his bag. "Oh, my beautiful Chana." He takes her in his arms just as the front door opens. He steps back to make way for Herschel.

"Layland, my boy. I want you to know that I will watch over your women while you are away," Herschel says. Herschel looks at Chana. "My goodness. How can you leave her?"

"It's killing me. I'm depending on you, Herschel."

"Chana and Amalie will be fine. You know how stubborn my mother is. She will come around."

"I hope so," sighs Layland. They both turn as Amalie walks down the stairs, dark braids encircling her head like a crown, and dressed in her new deep green chiffon. Herschel doesn't mean to gasp but the sound escapes involuntarily. Amalie didn't have time to form the myriads of tear-petals for her skirt but simply cut the entire dress on the bias. It flows down her lithe body like water, ending below her knees, her feet shod with the black strapped heels Layland picked out.

"Thank you for fabric," she says in stumbling English to Layland.

"Very good, Amalie," Herschel says.

"No worries. Me, Chana, we be ok," she tries to assure her brother-in-law.

Chana looks at her little sister proudly. She and Amalie had worked hard on those words. Grandmother Abbott enters and the air of happiness evaporates.

"Goodbye Grandson," she declares. "Your responsibilities will be waiting your return." She does not embrace him.

"Very well, Grandmother. Thank you for allowing Chana and Amalie to stay until then."

The older woman nods curtly. A driver raps at the door and Chana feels a welling panic. Amalie steps to her sister's side and holds her hand. Layland walks to Chana and pulls her head to his chest.

"I know you love the sea, but don't yo wish right now you loved it a little less?" asks Herschel.

Layland gulps and coughs. "I'll be back in two months, my darling." He kisses her on the top of her head, picks up his bag and walks out the door, Hershcel behind him.

Amalie holds Chana's hand. "Grandmother is watching you. Don't cry."

Chana inhales, her back and shoulder stiff and straight.

Grandmother Abbott points to Chana's dress. "That is a deceptive Emilio dress. Your feigned attempt to counterfeit an Italian designer is as fraudulent as you two gold-diggers. You may have deluded my grandson but I will root out your evil before he returns. You can't hide your true colors from me. Herschel will support me, as always—you'll see." She turns and climbs the stairs.

"I don't think she likes your dress," says Amalie.

Chana coughs, tears flowing. "I haven't felt this lonely since we left Kovno."

"Come on, let's change into our work dresses. I found a shed in the back that could use a good scrubbing. I think we can get it done before dinner."

"And tonight I sleep in an empty bed," says Chana.

"You can sleep with me while your husband is gone," says Amalie. "We'll braid our hair and talk about our family in Russia."

Chana hugs her sister.

The next morning the two sisters rise early and put on their patched Russian dresses. With Layland away, Herschel delays his departure to the bank so he can drive Chana and Amalie to school.

"I wish I knew enough English to tell Herschel we would rather walk," says Amalie.

I think we make him late for the bank," says Chana.

He opens the car door of his black Rolls Royce and motions to them. They obey his direction and get into the back seat. After their class, Herschel again waits for them and drops them at the doorstep of his mother's house. They enter quietly, put their school cases away, and busy themselves with cleaning every inch of the mammoth house. Today their new Grandmother does not stop their endeavors. As they work they chatter about their English classes, challenging one another.

"No, it's an eeeoooo sound," says Chana.

"I keep missing it. Why don't you try your English with Uncle Herschel?" asks Amalie. "You say many words better than me."

"Layland's grandmother disapproves of me," says Chana. "Practicing my English in front of her makes me nervous." Chana wrings out her cloth.

"I think she might be softening," says Amalie. "She let us clean today."

They put away their buckets and get the dusting cloths.

"Do you think Otto is back home?" Amalie asks.

"Of course. Grandfather said he would find him."

"Just the same, I'd like to hear from them," says Amalie. "We need to let them know where we are."

"Layland will talk with his friend in Estonia," says Chana. "His friend might have a contact in Russia. Layland will help us find our brother."

"It's almost five o'clock. We better bathe and prepare for dinner," says Amalie. "I finished our new dinner dresses last night. They're hanging in my room."

"Are they short?"

"Shorter than the other ones—they barely cover our knees."

"Herschel likes us," says Chana. "He used to be late, but now he comes home earlier and earlier. I think I'll fix your hair special tonight. I'll wear mine in twisted braids."

Chana, dressed in a mauve frock, ribboned at the cuffs, and Amalie, wearing a blue twist-dress with front tucks and tight bolero at the back, hurry to stand behind their chairs. Grandmother Abbott sits at the head of the table, wine glass in hand. Herschel pulls out the chairs for the young women and sits across from Amalie. Her eyes dance as she quietly mouths the "eeeoooo" sound.

Harriet serves the plates. Grandmother Abbott looks at the food, shoves it aside and pours another glass of wine.

Herschel smiles at Amalie and asks, "What is your name?"

Amalie takes a deep breath. "My na.."

"Oh, for Pete's sake," Grandmother Abbot interrupts. "Must we endure this nightly ritual?"

"Mother! We'll only get to know Chana and Amalie if they can converse with us, so we must help them learn English skills, or would you prefer to learn Russian?" He turns to Amalie again. "What is your name?"

Grandmother Abbott takes a belt from her glass.

"My name is Amalie Meinrel," she smiles. Her eyes sparkle in the candlelight. "I am from Kovno, Russia, a beeootiful Jewish commeeoooonity." She did it! The words were flawless. Chana squeezes her hand and Amalie beams – for a moment. She sees the fear in Herschel's eyes. He rushes to calm his mother.

Grandmother Abbott throws her wine glass onto the floor, shattering it. She stands up and shouts angry, quick words at her son, who tries to calm her. Amalie and Chana watch the exchange.

"I didn't know America hated Jews too," says Amalie.

"Layland doesn't," says Chana, wiping tears.

Grandmother Abbott stomps from the room.

Herschel motions for Amalie and Chana to follow him.

"I am sorry. My mother is afraid. She's from old blood. Again, I'm so sorry, but she won't allow you to stay."

Amalie nods and Chana holds her stomach and sobs. Amalie punches Chana's arm. Chana straightens but the tears flow down her cheeks.

"Bushta-budah! Come what may," Amalie spits. "We go." She blinks hard, presses her lips and sets her chin.

"I will take you to another house. It's ok," Herschel reassures in soft tones. "To a hotel – but just for a couple days. I will find a house – a nice house — one that Layland can afford on his salary and you can live there." He says the words slowly, hoping they understand.

Amalie blinks the moisture and touches Herschel's cheek with her cool palm. "Layland's Uncle Herschel says he will help us find another place to stay, I think."

Chana chokes. "Am I to leave my husband's home?"

Amalie runs a finger across Herschel's lined forehead. "Is all right, Herschel," she soothes.

Herschel sucks in air and holds it. His eyes fill with water. "You two young women are braver and stronger than my entire board of directors. Here you are in a foreign land, willing to be flung out to the streets with no way to communicate; no education or money, yet you stride forward with undauntable courage. No wonder Layland couldn't resist you. I wish my mother had a bigger heart. Go get your things. Hurry now." He gives hand signals. "Go get your things."

Chana and Amalie gather their belongings and re-join him at the door.

"Thank Grandmother Abbott," says Amalie.

Herschel nods, opening the door.


The three walk out of Grandmother Abbott's home. Herschel drives them to a hotel, arranges a suite, and gives detailed instructions to the manager to meet their other necessities. He requests a German interpreter, and uses the interpreter to talk with them, trying to arrange for their transportation to English classes and other activities. Amalie tells him firmly that they will walk to their school each morning. All too soon it is time for him to depart.

He regrets leaving them there.

He walks into his mother's opulent home, devoid of spirit. The grandeur sickens him. His mother descends the stairs and he can see she is titillated. She tries to engage him in justifying chit-chat about the deception of the Jewish harlots, but it repels him and he walks to the den, closes the large doors, and tries to lose his thoughts in the flames of the fireplace. How dead the house feels. After a while he ascends the staircase and climbs into bed. Behind his closed eyelids he can see Amalie's tear-filled eyes, and his mind won't stop focusing on Layland's expression when he has to tell him how his delicate wife was treated. At 4:00 a.m. Herschel gives up trying to sleep and drives to the bank. He looks through housing repossession files until he finds the right one. He completes the necessary paperwork and places it on his secretary's desk for typing. At 6:00 a.m. he telephones a contractor and arranges for repair, painting and cleaning. At 10:00 a.m. he waits outside the classroom of his two favorite Russians. He sees Amalie helping a young Asian woman with diction, and Chana waiting patiently nearby. When they see him they rush and embrace him.

Herschel laughs. "May I take you to brunch?" he asks.

Amalie purses her lips. "Bruch."

"No, brunnnch," he corrects.

"Brunnnch," she mimics, raising her eyebrows. "What is brunnnch?"

"Breakfast and Lunch – together it is brunch."

"Ahh," She turns to Chana and chatters.

"Ahh," says Chana.

"Yah, brunnnch we go," says Amalie.

Herschel helps them into the car and Amalie says something to Chana in German.

"What did you just say?" asks Herschel.

"I say, Herschel drive—never …," Amalie looks at Chana.

"Never walk," says Chana.

"Never walk," says Amalie.

"I daresen't think what the board would say if they saw me walking on the public streets of Chicago," says Herschel.

Herschel parks at the Hofbrau Restaurant and escorts Chana and Amalie inside. A host seats them and Herschel orders lamb burgers with tomato jam, potato frittata, and celery soup for the three of them. Chana and Amalie sip their soup and chatter, but don't touch the burgers or potatoes. The waitress looks at the untouched food.

"They're not as hungry as I thought," says Herschel. "Take it away." He reaches inside his jacket, pulls out a cigar and lights it. Amalie stares at his smoking lips. He blows smoke rings and she chatters to Chana, pointing at them, so he blows more and she smiles.

"Do you want to try it?" Herschel asks, holding out his cigar.

Amalie reaches for the cigar and Chana buries her elbow into her sister's ribs. Amalie holds the cigar like Herschel. He watches her place it between her lips and puff until her mouth is filled with smoke. She opens her mouth wide, allowing a portion of the smoke to escape, then closes her lips fast and tight to cut it off. A perfect circle rises, and Herschel laughs. Amalie laughs and sucks the smoke into her lungs and a fit of coughing ensues. She hands the cigar back to Herschel. Chana looks away, with perfect posture and tight lips and rolls her eyes.

"Come on," Herschel says. "I'll show you to the house I purchased for Layland."

Swerving through Chicago's busy streets, he can't stop himself from talking.

"It's only a bungalow, but it's in one of Chicago's nicest neighborhoods, and there's plenty of room inside for the three of you, even room for my great nieces and nephews, should I be so lucky, and the back yard is large—enough room for a garden and a play area. It's a sound investment even if Layland decides he doesn't want it. I got it for half the price. I put it right into Layland's name and made sure the payments are affordable on his salary."

He stops in front of the house. Two workmen hammer on the house in a constant rhythm. Another worker shovels at the corner where the porch joins, and a fourth stands up on the roof and watches them.

"Come on inside," says Herschel. "Be careful. The walls are wet with paint. They can't paint the exterior until summer."

Chana and Amalie look at each other and shrug.

"Chana – the house is for you and Layland – and Amalie too until she marries," explains Herschel. "Layland's house."

"Thank you, Ocle Herschel," smiles Amalie broadly. "Aye, good house."

"Good house," Chana says. "My husband's house."

Construction hammering drowns out their conversation and he motions to them. "We'll talk in the car on the way back to the hotel."

Herschel listens to the foreign chatter all the way back to the hotel, parks under the canopy, and walks the young women to their suite.

"You move to your new house next week," explains Herschel. "I will get your furniture arranged." The girls look puzzled so he repeats himself. "You will need to stay here until next week."

"We stay here? How long?" asks Amalie.

"You will move to the house in seven or eight days."

"Ahh, good," brightens Amalie. Chana nods.

"Thank you for brunch," Amalie spiels, proud to know the new word. "You come to new house – I cook. Ok?"

"Ok," he says smiling.

# CHAPTER 20
## *April 1921*

Fedora Meinrel steadies herself with her frozen feet—numb now and far less painful. How many months has she been on this death march? Five? No, six. Men, women and children surround her in the train's boxcar, many in worse shape and a few dead. She cannot fathom how long the train has been moving—days, minutes, weeks, hours. She hasn't slept for so long that everything feels distorted. She has no body fat and tries to remember the last time she felt warmth. An old woman sinks to her knees and Fedora grabs her arm and pulls her up. "Don't lie down," Fedora warns, pointing upward to the slats in the roof where soldiers sit. "They will shoot you." The woman leans against Fedora. "No, dear woman. You must stand on your own or die."

"Dying is all right with me," the woman says.

Fedora pushes her away. "Don't die yet. Perhaps tomorrow, but not yet."

The train slows down. "Another station where they offload the dead," mutters the old woman. The train stops and the door slides open. Fedora squints at the brightness.

"Everybody off," orders a soldier jerking people to the ground. Fedora cowers to the edge, not wishing to break a leg. She holds onto the door and jumps off the train. She looks back to help the old woman. A soldier yanks the old woman's skirt and she tumbles off the train into a heap. Fedora squats to examine her.

"Get in line," a soldier orders.

Fedora feels around the woman's ankle and she gasps in pain. Fedora rips a layer from her skirt.

"Get in line," the soldier orders again, cocking his gun. She feels the point of the gun barrel against her filthy, matted red hair, but continues wrapping the old woman's ankle. The sound of the bullet explodes.

Otto sits up. "Mama, Mama," he cries. "I have to go home." He dresses quickly in the darkness and descends the stairs. He quietly closes the front door behind him, hoping not to awaken his new mother, and sprints in the direction he knows will take him home.

Otto runs a good hour before he sees the first signs of light. He runs as much as he can throughout the day and doesn't stop that night. Before morning he sees Kovno, excitement pulsating through him. He tears across the back porch of his home, bursting through the door, startling his sleeping grandparents.

"Otto?" Galayna asks.

"Grandson!" Chingas says.

The two take their grandson into their arms, kissing his head and face.

Galayna gets up and throws her housedress over the top of her night clothes. "Grandson, why are you here?" she asks, wiping her tears.

"I had the dream you prayed for," says Otto, sniffling. "I saw my mother die. She was riding in a train. It was really crowded, people shoving against one another. Her hair was matted and she was cold and dirty. The train stopped and mother had to help an old woman. The soldier told her to get in line but she wanted to help the old woman. The soldier shot her. I saw it. I heard the gunshot." Otto sobs.

Chingas takes his grandson into his arms. Chingas hasn't stopped crying and now his shoulders shake.

Otto wipes his face on his sleeve and Chingas wipes his on his quilt.

"Grandfather, you are so thin. You look different."

"I know," says Chingas. "After I got your sisters to Bremen I made myself stay alive until I could find you. And here you are." Chingas's voice breaks.

"Are my sisters all right?" asks Otto.

Chingas blows his nose. "I'll tell you all about it on the way back to your Aunt Vyvyan's house," he says. "Help me up, Grandson."

"But, can't I stay here?" begs Otto.

"No, Otto. Lenin must never know you exist. He will ignore us two old skelatons, but you…" Chingas stops mid-sentence. "Galayna, we need to get on the road."

"No, Chingas, you can't! Your leg…"

Chingas interrupts her objections. "This is my prayer, Galayna. You have so many prayers but I've only had this one."

"Aye," Galayna says.

"We need to leave before anyone sees Otto. Is there bark bread? We can get water from the streams." Otto steadies Chingas while he dresses.

"I'm coming with you," Galayna says.

"You need to stay here and ward off questions," he says. "I'll get Otto to safety."

Galayna hands Chingas the bread. "You come back to me, Chingas," she orders.

He puts a shawl across his shoulders, grabs his walking stick, and guides Otto out the door.

"I haven't slept, Grandfather," Otto says.

"You're going to be plenty tired by the time you get home," Chingas says. "Have you tried riding the trees yet this spring? Your grandmother told me the story of how you escaped the Red Army."

"No, not yet. They're still too stiff. I fear the trees will die. The bark people are stripping the bark all the way around the trunk—not leaving any for the tree's nourishment."

"Yes, Otto. It's a shame. They're trading their futures for a mess of pottage."

"What?" asks Otto.

"It's a story your Grandmother tells. It's about a hungry man who trades his entire future inheritance for a handful of food. Satisfying immediate needs can be very costly."

"Like killing an entire tree just for a little bread today." says Otto.

"Yes."

"I must sleep tonight," says Otto.

"We'll see," says Chingas. "How long did it take you to get to Kovno?"

"My dream about mother woke me up. It was still dark and I snuck out of the house and started running. About an hour later I could see the beginning of daylight. I ran all day, then all that night until I saw you. I guess it was just yesterday before sunrise that I started running, but I haven't rested and I'm really tired."

"Vyvyan didn't know you left?" Chingas asks.

"No. She would have stopped me."

"I know you're tired, Grandson, but you'll have to press through."

"Tell me about my sisters," says Otto. "Where are they?"

For the rest of the day Otto listens to stories about the trek to Bremen.

"You need to remember the name of the ship, Otto."

"The S.S. Sierra Nevada," says Otto. "They got tickets to New York City, United States of America. I won't forget."

"You promised your grandmother you would find your sisters when you grow up, and I expect you will keep that promise."

"It's dark, Grandfather. I think I can find us a place to rest."

"No, Grandson, you must keep going. If you run you'll be able to stay awake and probably get home before noon tomorrow. I'm just slowing you down. We need to part ways now, Grandson."

Otto puts his arms around his grandfather. "Will you get back home all right?"

"Of course. Now let me see you run, Otto, and don't stop until you get home."

"I love you, Grandfather," Otto yells over his shoulder.

"Thank you for saving your sisters," Chingas shouts. "I love you Otto," he whispers. His chin is quivering. "Thank you, God."


"OH, OTTO! I WAS SICK WITH WORRY!" Vyvyan is vexed. "Anatoly could be here any minute. Quickly, let's get you bathed and changed."

Vyvyan yanks and jerks Otto's clothing, throws him in cold bathwater, and doesn't cover his eyes when she rinses his hair. She ignores his modesty as she runs a washcloth over every inch of his grimy body, then dresses him in his new uniform.

"I'm very tired, mother," he says.

She smiles at him. "I bet you don't get out of bed tonight."

She prepares mountains of food as Otto sets the table. Anatoly arrives at five and the three sit down to eat. Otto uses his utensils flawlessly. His eyes droop and his head feels too heavy.

"Vyvyan, our son is asleep in his food," Anatoly complains.

Vyvyan laughs. "That he is!"

Anatoly carries Otto up the stairs and lays him in bed and Vyvyan covers him with a blanket.

# CHAPTER 21
## *Spring 1921*

At dawn Layland steps from the train's platform, and hails a taxi. A block before he sees his Grandmother's house he rolls down the window to look down the street. He wants to catch Chana before she leaves for her English classes. He over-pays the driver, runs up the walk, leaps to the top step and turns the latch.

"Chana!" he yells bursting into the house, switching on a light. "Chana, I'm home." He drops his bags and fumbles with his overcoat."

Clicking footsteps run from the kitchen.

"Master Jarmon!" Harriet exclaims.

"Hello Harriet. Chana hasn't left for school yet, has she?"

"You will need to discuss that with your grandmother," balks Harriet, turning on her heel and retracing her steps back to the kitchen.

"Layland! Welcome home," calls his grandmother descending the stairs.

"Grandmother, where is Chana?"

"Please, Layland. You cannot still be harboring feelings for that trollop. You obviously know nothing about her."

"Grandmother! Where is my wife?"

"I don't know. Herschel helped me dispatch them when they announced they were Jews. Really, Layland. Did you have to dig to the bottom?"

"What?"

"Don't yell, Layland. You'll cause me to have a headache. I know what a shock it must be. She should have told you. Don't worry. I took care of it." His Grandmother ignores her smoldering grandson and reaches to the wall and pulls a cord. Harriet appears instantly. "Harriet, take my Grandson's things to his room."

"Don't touch them, Harriet," Layland fumes. "I won't be staying. Grandmother, where is Herschel?" Layland dons his coat and hat.

"Probably at the bank. He practically lives there. Must you leave so soon? You barely got here. Surely you can have breakfast with me."

"I trusted you to take care of her, Grandmother," Layland levels darkly. He turns away from her, picks up his bag and leaves.

Layland arrives at the bank almost two hours before it opens. He sprints up the marble steps leading to the double, gilt doors and pulls the handles, but they are locked. He shakes them, sending raucous clattering sounds into the hushed morning. He listens at the doors and hears nothing, so he bangs loudly. "Uncle Herschel! Are you in there? Herschel! It's Layland. Let me in!" Within seconds Layland hears keys jangling in the locks and his uncle opens the door.

"Layland!"

"Where are they," Layland erupts, dispelling the pleasantries.

"Chana and Amalie? Didn't you get my cable?"

"No, but I want to see them now," Layland almost yells.

Herschel places both hands on Layland's shoulders. "Layland, I bought you a house, and moved Chana and Amalie into it. They're happy." He pushes Layland back out the door and locks up. "Come on. Let's go to them. They will be in class by now, but Chana will be thrilled to see you."

Layland hugs Herschel. "I am sorry for the tirade. I was just so… Chana is just so… Well, I thank you. I should have known you would watch over them. Your mother said they had been dispatched and I panicked."

"I fully understand. Come. Hop into my car. It will hold all of us."

"Does Chana have furnishings for the house?" asks Layland.

"Yes the house is fully furnished, although the most important appointment seems to be Otto's hat. It's the only item on the mantel except for the two candles that flank it."

"One of these days I'm going to bring that boy home and surprise Chana," says Layland.

Herschel swerves around a corner. "Just a few more blocks," he says.

"Uncle, I don't suppose I can request a favor."

"Name it," Herschel says.

"Well, Chana and I haven't had time alone since we were married – none to speak of anyway. And I like the idea of being in our own home."

Herschel looks out the window at a broken-down trolley.

"I just thought you might like to take Amalie for a meal and perhaps show her around the bank, etcetera, etcetera," Layland exaggerates the syllables.

"I would love to do that. She hasn't seen but few of the sites. I'm trying to think of an excuse to postpone the board meeting, but she may just have to accompany me. It would be my pleasure to entertain Amalie. May I have her all night? There's a play I think she would relish, and then I'll book her into the presidential suite of our hotel. Don't worry about her clothing. It will be a good excuse to force her into buying something."

"You are a prince," says Layland. "There's the school. Pull in behind that cab."

Herschel parks behind a taxi and Layland instructs the cabby to wait.

"This way," says Herschel. "They changed classrooms."

The men stride into the school, climb the steps and stand outside the classroom watching Chana and Amalie repeating phrases after their teacher, exaggerating their lips and tongues. As Amalie turns to Chana her eyes freeze on the door. Chana looks at the doorway. Both girls stare, daring not to dash from their class.

The professor sees the situation. "Class dismissed," he announces. The girls arise, pick up their books, and with restrained decorum walk out the door. In the hallway Chana bursts into Layland's arms and their grasp and kisses continue as Herschel escorts Amalie to his car.

"How long can you stay?" asks Chana.

"At least a month," says Layland. "We're in the Barnnacle bay."

Chana looks at Amalie. "I won't be going to English class while Layland is home."

Amalie looks at Herschel. "Don't worry about Chana's classes. She's the smartest student. It will give the rest of us a chance to catch up to her."

"You can't walk to school by yourself," says Herschel.

Amalie shrugs. "Why not? Soon I will tell you in English about all my walking."

"I'll drive you. These Chicago streets aren't that safe."

"Chana and Layland should be alone. Can you take me to bank with you?" Amalie asks.

"Of course," says Herschel. "Afterwards we'll have some fun. I'll show you the world's first sky-scraper made out of structural steel."

Amalie shrugs.


Three weeks later Herschel waits in his car for Amalie to finish her English class. He checks his pocket watch. "It's time for you to be done, little Miss Amalie." He cranes his neck to see the door and spots her, talking with another student. She's wearing a navy-blue sailor dress, which she wasn't wearing when he dropped her at school. He jumps out and opens the passenger door for her.

"Who is that Asian girl you were talking with?" he asks, pulling away from the curb.

"My friend, Jing," she says.

"Not your friend, your acquaintance," he says. "Ac-quaint-ance."

"Ac-quaint-ance," she mimicks.

"Weren't you wearing your peasant dress when I dropped you off?"

Amalie arches her brows.

"Your dress is different," he says.

"My ac-quaint-ance make new dress for me."

"Remarkable. She sewed it? It's absolutely smashing."

"I teach my ac-quaint-ance to sew. She got job. She sew me dress."

"No, no, no," Herschel says. "Someone who makes something personal for you cannot be just an acquaintance."

Amalie tilts her head.

Herschel sighs. "Jing is your friend, whether I like it or not." He stops in front of Layland's new house. "Here we are." He gets out, opens her door and walks her to the porch.

"Come in. I cook borscht and bread."

"I have a board meeting, but I'll be by this evening at the usual time." He laughs. "The usual time means that I spend every minute I have here with you, Chana and Layland. No wonder I'm so happy."

Amalie kisses his cheek. "See you at usual time."

Herschel smiles all the way back to his car.


After dinner Herschel clips two cigars, puts them in his breast pocket, and walks to the front porch with Layland. Herschel offers a cigar and Layland runs it under his nose and puts it between his lips. Herschel flicks his lighter and Layland leans into it. They stand quietly puffing.

"Spring is my favorite time to be in Chicago," says Layland.

"Chana is happiest when you are home, whatever the climate," Herschel says.

"I know. When I'm captain I'll have my own quarters and can take her with me," says Layland. "We talk about it all the time. It's our dream to sail together. But for now I wish she had something that challenged her more than her English classes."

"There's a medical school nearby. She used to be a doctor— at least her mother was," says Herschel.

"Perhaps when she masters the language we can go to medical school," says Layland.

"I talked with Rabbi Lowenstein again," says Herschel.

"Did he find out anything about Otto?" Layland asks.

"Maybe. He got word to his sources in Russia, and they found out that Kovno was sacked very close to the time that the girls left — maybe within hours. The grandparents were barely alive – starving to death. The report on the parents was grim. There was a mass grave. The grandparents were asked about Otto but they denied knowing him. When the neighbors were questioned one villager said she saw him a few days after the Cheka's massacre."

"Wow! Did you tell the girls?"

"Rabbi Lowenstein told them. They cried when they heard of their parents, but were happy their grandfather made it home. When the rabbi told them about Otto being spotted in Kovno they sobbed with relief. They never ask for anything but they hugged me. I gave money to Rabbi Lowenstein for their grandparents. The rabbi says he doubts it will reach them. He worries for the safety of his contact."

The men puff until Layland breaks the silence. "Those grandparents will never divulge Otto's whereabouts. If it were my grandson I'd get him to safety. Are there any other relatives?"

"I thought of that too," agrees Herschel. "The girls said their grandmother has a half-sister. She's much younger—Aunt Vyvyan. I was going to trace that lead but I stopped because the rabbi feared for Otto's safety. We need information about his circumstances before we proceed."

"Maybe there's another resource that can help us," says Layland.

"Another resource?"

"I was able to get a Russian contact through my friend in Estonia. They trap in Siberia and have a good network throughout Russia. I pick up their furs in Estonia every spring. I just picked up their crate and delivered it to Germany so I won't see them again until next year. They've become friends and I trust them. Maybe they could help us. I worry about the Rabbi's network—it might be over-exposed."

"Rabbi Lowenstein is a wise man. He told me about all the rabbis who have died in Russia. I have another appointment with him tomorrow—I'd love it if you and the girls came along."

"Thanks, we will. I'm sure we'll all have questions."

"The girls have met with the rabbi several times about their Jewish heritage. He's also an immigrant and very patient with their questions. Right now they're quizzing him about how to be both Christian and Jewish, since their mother was Christian." Herschel smiles. "You should see them chattering in the back seat. I'd give anything to understand what they're saying."

"Is that possible to be both Christian and Jewish?" asks Layland.

"It's not a new concept and the rabbi is a good listener."

"Chana hasn't talked with me at all about her heritage except to say that they couldn't practice it in Russia. She prays every night—something her mother and grandmother did. There were pogroms in place, and they were forbidden to worship under penalty of death, but she said they never stopped praying."

"I cannot imagine what it took for their parents to keep them safe in that furnace of hate. They're not even singed," Herschel says, studying his cigar.

"Chana is," corrects Layland. "She gets quiet. I know her heart is full of heavy thoughts, but she seems afraid to share them with me, and Grandmother Abbott didn't help matters." They both take puffs on their cigars and watch the orange fluorescence. "I wish Chana knew that I count myself the luckiest man in the world, being in the right place at the right time. I've traveled to every country to find her."

"You are a very lucky man, Lay. You have done well."

"And so are you, Uncle."

"Yes, the bank is doing well, but it's not worth the fortune you've struck."

"I wasn't talking about the bank," says Layland.

"Ah, well, yes," he admits looking at the house. "I love this house. It suits you and Chana. It's fortunate it was available."

"I wasn't talking of the house either, but as long as you mention it, I was going to offer you a room. After all, you are here every possible moment."

"Sorry, Layland. I know I've been here too much."

"Actually, not enough according to Amalie. When are you going to wake up and ask her to marry you?"

Herschel studies his nephew. "It must be obvious. I think of the irony of it – the perfect companions, born in the wrong decades. She's eighteen. I am thirty-one — thirteen years her senior!"

"Twelve and a half," says Layland.

The men suck on their cigars.

"I'm smitten, there is no doubt," Herschel admits. "She is one of the brightest minds I've ever met – much too smart to accept a proposal from me. And her magnetism – I've known the most sophisticated women in society and none could match her. I want to make her happy more than I want to breathe. I bought her a house, too."

"No! You bought her a house?"

"A big one. Something her entire village can live in and never run into one another. Of course, it's an excellent investment, but I had a more compelling reason driving me to purchase it. But now I fear telling her about it."

"I feel compelled to encourage you, dear Uncle," Layland says.

"It's new territory for me," Herschel says. "I've never felt happier, yet I'm always confused. I don't know how to take the next step."

"What did you do when you decided to start an investment bank and you needed charters?"

"I got them. I needed them, and, it took a little convincing, but I finally got them."

"Well. Isn't this the same thing?"

"Not even close."

"Why?"

"Because I could have recovered if they had refused the bank's charter. If Amalie rejects me, my soul will be lost. It's high risk."

Layland puts his hand on Herschel's shoulder. "I understand the gravity of your concern, Uncle, but I'll share with you something the girls are always saying when things seem extra difficult. It's what their parents said before they sent them away from Kovno to protect them from the murdering Cheka. They say, 'It's a risk, but a risk worthy to be taken.'"

"A risk worthy to be taken," Herschel repeats slowly.

"I think she loves you. You won't know how she feels for certain until you ask. She's an honest woman and won't be coy. If she loves you, she will tell you. As a married man I assure you, it is a risk worthy of being taken, even if it costs your soul."

Herschel extinguishes his cigar. A light breeze distills the air.

"Come with me, nephew. I don't want to put this off a moment longer, but I don't want to frighten her by saying words that she might not fully understand. To tell you the truth, I have scarcely thought of anything else. Perhaps she will not feel fear if you and Chana are close by."

Chana and Amalie face each other on the settee in the living room, conversing quietly as Amalie sews. Layland walks to Chana and takes her hand. She rises and he leads her to the edge of the room. Herschel approaches Amalie and bows before her and takes a large breath. His heart pounds so loudly he worries she can hear it.

"Amalie Meinrel. I love you." He allows the words to escape before his courage wanes. His high-pitched voice quivers.

Amalie stops sewing and looks at Herschel.

"Yah?" she says raising her eyebrows.

"Yah – yes. Yes, Amalie; I love you and I want to be your husband."

"Yah?"

"Amalie, do you understand what I am asking?"

"I understand." She holds up her work. "Do you see what I make?" she asks softly.

Herschel focuses on the myriads of white lace.

"It is dress to marry a very good man – Herschel Abbott," she whispers.

Tears well in Herschels eyes but he can't look away.

Amalie places her long white index finger over his gaping mouth. "Almost too much lace. Is good you ask." She arches her brows. "I wait and wait and sew and sew." She sets her sewing aside, looks into his eyes and wraps his face in her cool palms, pushing in his cheeks and squishing his lips a little too much, but he doesn't stop her. "I love you, Herschel," she says. She kisses him and when they open their eyes, he stands and brings her to him, folding her small body in his large arms.

Layland and Chana embrace.

Amalie unexpectedly pulls back from Herschel. "You must ask Mother Abbott to wedding."

Herschel sighs. "Oh boy." He draws Amalie closer.

# CHAPTER 22
## *June 17, 1921*

Herschel's designer, Genevieve, talks on the phone.

"How many gardenias and white roses?" asks the florist.

"Mr. Abbott will need ten thousand," says Genevieve. "And he'll need another ten thousand red roses. Can you handle that order?"

"When do you need them?"

"Tomorrow."

"We can provide the flowers, but it will require extra commercial flights from both New York and San Francisco."

"Call me right back with the costs so I can send you a draft." Genevieve hangs up and turns to Herschel.

"The flowers will cover the entire exterior stairway and we'll carry the floral theme throughout the house, including the master suite. The interior stairway and balcony will be decked with identical flowers. I'll have an alter placed in the library for Judge Iverson. I'll frame the alter with painted trees and branches, all of which will have flowers and crystals threaded generously in the branches. It's a simple design, sir, but it will be beautiful."

"What about Amalie's bouquet?" asks Herschel.

"She and Chana have consented to wear floral crowns, but they don't want to carry flowers."

"And the dining table? And dinner?"

"I'll place decorated branches in the center of the table. It will allow conversation, and the sparkling branches will give a cozy feeling. I'll fill the branches with flowers, hang streams of crystals, and place heavy bouquets around the base. Each place setting will be in pure crystal stemware, crystal plates, crystal bowls, and goldware. I'll use red table coverings and drapes. Again, sir, it will sparkle with simple beauty and smell glorious."

"Table?" asks Herschel, glancing around. "When are you expecting the furniture delivery?"

"Any time, now, sir. It wasn't easy to find the perfect furnishings for an entire mansion, but I have an excellent purchasing department. Your mansion will be magnificent, sir."

"It isn't a mansion."

"Well, congratulations on purchasing such a superb property."

"It's my wife's wedding gift. Did you give the caterer my instructions?"

"Yes. Everything is being prepared. How many guests did you say?"

"Ten, but now you will prepare for nine."

"Twenty thousand flowers and nine guests?"

"Yes."

"May I ask who declined the invitation, sir?"

"My mother, thank goodness."

The exterior bell rings.

"That will be the furnishings, sir. May I be excused?"


THROUGH THE NEXT forty-eight hours Genevieve and fifty of her employees furnish and decorate Amalie's new home with efficiency, precision and beauty.

THE MORNING OF June 17, 1921, a limousine stops in front of Amalie's Oak Park home on Chicago Avenue. The driver opens the door and helps Amalie and Chana to the sidewalk. They look at the railing and arched entry, thick with flowers.

"Herschel likes flowers," Amalie says. "I will need very big garden."

They walk up the steps and through the front door.

"This way, please," says Genevieve. "I have your flowered crowns in the powder room."

"Just a minute," says Amalie.

"What's wrong?" asks Genevieve.

"Turn, Chana. I want to check your dress."

Chana turns, her muted-purple, off-shoulder, floor-length chiffon gown moving with her like liquid.

"What a magnificent dress," says Genevieve. "Who's the designer?"

"Me," says Amalie. "How's my dress?" She turns slowly.

Genevieve touches the lace. "Oh, my, the lace is so lightweight. Where on earth did you find it? Paris?"

"I needled it," says Amalie. Amalie's dress bodice of fitted lace matches the lacy layers of her floor-length skirt, finished with a rose-colored satin sash emphasizing her tiny waist and a rose-colored satin under-slip.

"You both look absolutely stunning," says Genevieve. "Should we get your crowns?"

Chana whispers to Amalie in Russian. "Remember the crowns grandfather put on our heads, Amalie?"

Amalie sighs. "'As beautiful as Queen Esther,' grandfather said. Yes, I remember. I miss all of them."

They follow Genevieve into the powder room. "This is Rolf," she says. "He will work the flowers into your hairstyles."

"Sit, sit," says Rolf. "Such beautiful black hair—the perfect color for white flowers. We do the bride first. I like the way your hair is pulled to one side in a profusion of black curls. We can make it seem that it springs from a circle of gardenias and ribbons, see? So beautiful. And the bridesmaid, with hair pulled high—a crown of flowers, yes?"

"Are you ready?" asks Genevieve. "The harpist has given the signal for entrance music. Chana, you will be the first to walk into the library. Walk very slowly, like this." Genevieve demonstrates. "When you get to the podium you will move to the left, opposite your husband, turn slightly like this and look expectantly to your sister. Do you understand?"

"Yes," says Chana."

"Amalie, you will wait until Chana reaches the front and turns to look at you, and then you will slowly walk in. Should I show you how to walk?"

Amalie smiles. "No."

"So, do you both understand?"

They nod.

"Come, Chana and Amalie. It's time. No. Wait, wait, Amalie. No, not yet." Genevieve reaches to stop them but misses.

Chana and Amalie walk down the aisle, holding hands, smiling at their men. Herschel and Layland look at each other and breathe deep, tears in their eyes.

# CHAPTER 23
## *October 30, 1921*

Anatoly Kazakov has been hiking for three hours to be on time for the tête-à-tête. He kicks his way through dripping ferns, the spongy ground under his feet giving way like thick carpet while birch trees overhead hang onto the last of their yellowed leaves. He ignores all of it. Anatoly knows that the Watch Chief of Lenin's subordinate staff is already there waiting; he can smell his cigarette smoke before he spots the ambitious youth. He knows the young officer wants to prove himself and probably tastes a sweet promotion. Anatoly watches him throw down his cigarette and twist it under his boot.

"Hail, Commissar" he blurts. Anatoly raises his head to acknowledge, keeping his right hand on the gun's backstrap in his pocket. He walks closer and closer until he is within inches of the soldier's face. The youth plants his feet, allowing the closeness.

"Who knows you are here, Yakolev?" Anatoly demands.

"No one, sir, I assure you – except my driver, of course."

Anatoly steps back a few inches and studies the chief. The young man is dressed meticulously; he's tall and self-assured. Anatoly can see that Yakolev is comfortable with himself. "Tell me what you found," he orders.

Yakolev has been anticipating this moment. His information will please the commissar.

"The boy was delivered to your home by an old woman – Galayna Meinrel. She is Jewish. Her family has lived in Kovno for generations. Unfortunately, the Cheka raided last year, trampling all leads. Most of the village is dead. The old woman and her husband were the only ones from the family that survived the raid. I couldn't find their connection to Ilya, but I found one to Vyvyan. It seems that Galayna and Vyvyan have the same father. Ilya was Vyvyan's stepfather. I haven't yet clarified the connection between the birth of the boy and Vyvyan's half-sister. There was an inquiry from America about the boy."

"Inquiry from America?"

"Yes. A nearby villager went into Kovno and paid for information about a red-haired boy, Otto's age. It seems there are relatives in America looking for him."

"What village? Do you know the name of the questioner?"

"Rotchev. The questioner was a Rabbi from Kuverna."

Anatoly chews on this new piece of information. Yakolev interrupts his thoughts. "I'll be getting more on that over the next few weeks," he reassures. I have spies watching the rabbi.

Anatoly is irked at the blundering Yakolev. "Who is your source?"

"One of the peasants in Rotchev. They'll do anything for a loaf of bread," says Yakolev reaching for another cigarette.

"Did you dispatch the peasant couple – the Meinrels?" he asks.

Yakolev smirks confidently. "No need. They were walking skeletons. They're dead by now."

The firing bullet from Anatoly's gun shatters the silence as it enters Yakolev's body, destroying his heart while Yakolev attempts to form words.

"NO NEED," Anatoly sneers disgustedly.

Anatoly hikes back through the woods toward the road. Yakolev's car is running and he uses his gun to encourage the driver into the woods. Ignoring the pleas, Anatoly pulls the trigger and the man slumps to the ground. He leaves the bodies where they have fallen and hastens back to Yakolev's vehicle. Anatoly drives to the outskirts of Moscow where his borrowed automobile is secluded. Good. No one has discovered it. Family risks require greater secrecy than political ones. He abandons Yakolev' car, leaving it running, climbs into his own, and drives away. Marauders will strip Yakolev's car and by the time its shell is identified, people will have stopped questioning his whereabouts.

Another village to be erased. Actually two. If there is an American connection to Otto he will find it. And erase it. Anatoly is predictable about only one thing: He consistently trades out work crews and confidants with clean dispatch. No one person has the history or future plans of his dealings.

Anatoly broods as he drives. Vyvyan has lied to him, and somehow she has included the boy in her conspiracy. It's not surprising to him since she has been overly solicitous. Of course, the news that Vyvyan is not Ilya's daughter is old information, but it is information he will not share with the likes of Yakolev. It had been interesting to Anatoly to watch the lengths Ilya would go in order to protect his lie. Ilya actually used his wife as collateral to force Vyvyan, his step-daughter, into marriage, and the pretense had worked delightfully to Anatoly's benefit. He had admired Vyvyan since she was a child and bargaining for her hand in marriage was entertaining and rewarding. Ilya's secrets became his points of vulnerability.

Now Vyvyan and Otto share a secret that forces an invisible barrier around them. Anatoly will profit from their deception. Secrets require that people isolate themselves from those who would bring them or their loved ones harm. Even though Vyvyan's charm is sought at political events and parties, she keeps would-be friends at a distance. Otto prefers a dormitory room in the faculty area, away from fellow comrades.

Anatoly lets himself snicker aloud at the paradox: Vyvyan isolates herself to protect Otto and Otto isolates himself to protect Vyvyan. Let them have their secrets. He has a perfect family.

# CHAPTER 24
## *May 1922*

"Herschel, you must not fuss. I am fine," implores Amalie with both hands planted firmly on her back, her round stomach protruding generously under the volumes of brown cotton skirting. "Go to bank. I still be here doing this when you come home."

Herschel is unconvinced, so Chana supports her sister's position. "First babies come slowly," offers Chana. "It is fine."

Herschel looks haggard. It's only 8 a.m. but Amalie has had random pains all night. "Amalie," he pleads, "if only you would allow me to get Dr. Lawson here."

Amalie's face changes expressions and he can read the stubbornness. "Ok if your friend come," she concedes, "but he will not see my body."

Herschel blows a long breath to begin negotiating yet again. "Amalie, my beautiful round wife, he's a doctor. It's all right for doctors to deliver babies."

He can tell that she will not budge on this point so he turns to see if Chana will support him. Chana's face is kindly, as always. "Chana, won't you help me explain to your sister the difference between a man and a doctor?" Chana tilts her head as if expecting more information.

Amalie waddles to her husband.

"Amalie," Herschel implores. "Walter is one of my dearest and oldest friends. You met him when you and Chana lived at my mother's house. Remember? He lived next door. He has delivered many babies."

"Herschel," soothes Amalie. "Chana and me, we know about babies. We help mother in Kovno deliver the babies. Is private matter for women, so you go to work."

Herschel reaches for his hat, smooths his balding head, and places the derby firmly over the baldness. "Did she win?" he mumbles. His hands are still on his derby. He stands straighter, removes his hat, places it back on the tree and turns to face his wife.

"Amalie, I will not leave you today. I can have that law clerk, Sam Porter, bring me the documents and I can go through them here." He walks to the telephone and rings the bank, then rings the home of his life-long friend, Walter Lawson. When he lays the receiver down Amalie is standing there, straight and stormy. "I can be just as determined as you," he says. "Walter is coming, Amalie. If everything is all right, we will just sit here and play cards and he will not enter the bedroom. If Chana feels anything is not normal, he will be here to help."

"Aye," snaps Amalie. "He come and put his hands on me, and God look down and get very mad, and give us ugly baby! Herschel Abbott; he NOT..." Amalie grabs the molding trim surrounding the doorway, gasping in pain.

Herschel encircles her with his left arm around her back, lifting her slightly off the ground, and steers her to the bedroom. Chana hurries ahead of them to prepare the bed.

An hour later Amalie systematically writhes in pain while Herschel wipes her face. Chana stands near the window, her arms folded and her expression calm.

"You say this situation is natural, but it feels anything but natural," Herschel says. "I feel totally drained."

"It will be all right, Herschel," Chana says. "I pray."

Amalie moans and convulses.

"There, there, sweetheart, squeeze my hands," Herschel says, feeling her grip tighten around his fingers. "You are a powerfully strong woman." In the middle of the spasm, the doorbell chimes. Chana moves to the end of the bed to probe Amalie's progress. When she is finished Herschel reads the clouds in her soft eyes, and he knows she is worried.

When Amalie's grip relaxes Herschel runs to answer the door. "Please let it be Walt," he prays.

He opens the door. "Thank goodness!"

Dr. Walter Lawson is slightly shorter and stouter than Herschel. His thick brownish hair is disheveled as it has been since the days of their childhood. He wears eyeglasses and has a thick mustache, but is otherwise clean-shaven. Walter hands Herschel his bag and shakes off his coat. Herschel nods toward the coat rack, but is distracted by the opening front door. It's Herschel's mother. She removes her cape and short-brimmed hat and gives them to Herschel. She is regally bedecked in a dark poet's skirt, large-sleeved white blouse and pearls. This is her first visit and her eyes sweep the room, taking in all the elements.

"Mother!"

"Herschel, you look awful!"

"But, mother, why, how did you…" Herschel looks at Walter, with accusation.

"She's on my telephone party line," Walter explains.

"And it is a good thing," trumpets Mother Abbott. "How else would I hear about my grandchild?"

"Mother, please," urges Herschel. "Amalie is having a difficult time. Please go. I will call you after the child comes." Herschel sniffs. "Mother, gin already?"

"Stop it, Herschel," she orders. "Father McKay will be here shortly."

"What! Mother, you cannot be serious."

"No grandchild of mine will languish in sin while I have breath. Don't worry, Herschel. We'll keep the baptism quiet."

"Mother, Amalie and I have discussed this. Neither of us are staid in our beliefs and we want our child to find his own way." Herschel can hear Amalie moaning from the bedroom.

The doorbell rings and Mother Abbott answers it and ushers in Father McKay. Behind the good Father is Sam Porter, Herschel's law clerk.

Amalie screams as the pains crescendo, and all the attention in the entryway is riveted toward the bedroom. The doctor picks up his bag and rushes down the hallway with Mother Abbott at his heels and the Father obediently behind. Herschel tosses the coats toward the closet and scurries after them. "Wait, no, no, please don't…" he calls, but Walter is already entering the wailing room and Mother Abbott ignores her pecking son. Sam Porter follows the procession, hoping for a moment of Herschel's time.

Amalie sees the small congregation enter her birthing room. "Nooooooo," Amalie yells toward the intruders. "Herschel!"

Herschel runs to her and rings the water from her cloth and applies it to her forehead. She is gripped in the jaws of hell and cannot form words, but the second it begins to subside she grabs the front of her husband's shirt and brings his face directly into hers. "Herschel Abbot!" she blazes with clinched teeth. Before she can chastise him another spasm rips through her body, rendering her helpless.

As the pain crests Chana steps aside to allow the doctor to examine her sister. His look of concern confirms her findings. The doctor washes his hands in the basin and beckons Herschel to the side of the room.

"The baby is in breach position," explains Walter. "I doubt she can deliver without surgery."

"Surgery!" Herschel says. He starts to ask a question but his voice chokes.

"Herschel, I wish I could give you more comfort but the procedure is not new. We open the womb surgically and remove the baby."

Herschel must focus on this information. "I'm a banker, Walt. You need to give me numbers."

"Last year we were able to save nine of the fifteen women who had to go through this procedure. If we keep Amalie in the hospital longer, chances are she will survive."

"Nine out of fifteen? That's sixty percent!" shouts Herschel.

Amalie moans at the onset of another series of hard contractions. Chana wipes her face with a towel and smooths her dark locks against the white linen. Amalie's coloring is almost the same as the linen, except for the blotches of purple on her face and neck where veins have burst under the strain.

Herschel waits until Amalie's languishing diminishes, and rinses the cloth again, and wipes her face. He sees tears in her accusing eyes. "Amalie, you weren't compromised, I promise," he says.

She pulls the blankets over her face and cries. Walt pats Herschel's back.

"I've never felt such contradicting priorities," Herschel says, rinsing the cloth in the basin. "It isn't to that point yet, though, right Walt?"

"I'm sorry, Herschel. I think we should move her to the hospital right now."

Herschel involuntarily breathes out and in too quickly, and a sob breaks from his throat. "She wanted to have our…" his voice cracks. "…our baby in our bed."

"She's just not big enough to deliver a breach, Herschel. She'll need her strength if she's to survive the surgery. We shouldn't wait."

Herschel buries his face in both his palms.

Walter, Mother Abbott, Sam Porter and Father McKay form a loose huddle and Walt explains Amalie's peril.

"Humph. That figures," says mother Abbott. She huffs from the room, leaving four stunned men and two insulted young women.

Another pain grips Amalie and she faints.

"At least she isn't in pain," Walt says. "We need to revive her. Chana, apply the salts."

Mother Abbott returns with a bottle of Vodka and a glass. "You have nothing to drink in the den. I found this under the sink," she says.

Herschel kneels beside Amalie and takes her hand.

"Amalie, we need to take you to the hospital where we can help you and the baby a little better," Walt explains.

Amalie sobs.

"I'm sure a hospital would be more sanitary," Mother Abbott says, looking around.

"Mother, please!" Herschel says. "Must you be so…Can't you be nice even when Amalie…even now?"

Amalie jerks her hand from Herschel's and wipes her face on her sheet. She stops crying and, although pale, her eyes are full of fire. She chatters to Chana breathlessly in German, then turns to the doctor.

"I have baby here," she proclaims as another pain engulfs her. When she can breathe again she blurts orders to Walt, the words emerging from her mouth in staccato-like screams amidst her writhing. "You pull it out — pull out baby – it come NOW."

The doctor obediently checks the progress and shakes his head apologetically. "I'm sorry, Amalie. There is no change."

"Who is in charge—get this drama to a hospital where something useful can be done," says Mother Abbott to Father McKay. She sips from the glass then holds it up to inspect it.

"Father McKay, you look completely frozen. You haven't even breathed."

The priest doesn't move.

Mother Abbott fills her glass again.

"Chana! Help me push baby out," Amalie says. "Please, doctor. Please try again," she begs.

The doctor walks to Amalie and wipes her face with a damp cloth. "Amalie, my dear. You're so weak, I don't think…"

A contraction belts Amalie and she grabs Walt's sleeve and screams toward him. "Weak! Nya! Pull baby!" She releases his shirt and yells for her sister. "Chana – push! You remember. You do it!"

Chana moves to Amalie's stomach, waiting for inner promptings to direct her hands. Herschel positions himself at Amalie's bedside to hold her through the pain, and the doctor moves to the bottom of the bed. Chana places her hands at the top of the heap of stomach, just underneath Amalie's breasts. She applies deliberate pressure, encouraging the mammoth lump to turn during the height of the contraction.

"Chana, that made a difference. At the next round, do that again, only much harder."

The movement of the baby's twisting body into the birth canal causes a chain-reaction of torturous spasms and Amalie screams until she passes out.

"Father McKay, get the ammonia from my bag," yells Walt. The doctor complies, wetting a piece of cotton and running it under Amalie's nose. She immediately regains consciousness.

The ammonia odor causes Amalie's dizziness to subside, but a continuous enveloping pain requires her to push beyond her limits.

"Amalie, push," encourages the doctor.

"Come on, sweetheart," praises Herschel.

Amalie strains to comply until she withers and lapses into a haze. Walt keeps yelling at Father McKay to administer ammonia, Herschel talks calmly to Amalie through his blubbering, and Amalie's eyes roll back and her body relaxes. The ammonia is swept under her nose again, and then Father McKay takes a whiff. Amalie jolts back into consciousness.

Mother Abbot walks over to her son and looks down at her sweaty, writhing daughter-in-law and smirks. "Slav!" she says, and she walks to the far end of the room.

Herschel sees the fire ignite in Amalie's eyes.

"Help me, Herschel. Sit me up," she whispers hoarsely. Herschel sits her up, bracing her against his chest. "Slav, nya!" Amalie gives a mighty heave while Chana climbs on top of her sister and pushes against the twisted knot, and Walt pulls. Baby Abbott frees himself from his mother's body and Amalie falls back onto Herschel, limp.

"I've got it!" yells Walt. "I've got it!"

Herschel wipes Amalie's face and hair, soothing her with sweet words of love and praise in a squeaky, high-pitched, tearful voice, but her eyes stay closed.

A baby's cry rips the air and Herschel's arms encircle her, sobbing. He looks at Walt holding the slimy purple little body, squirming and screaming.

"It's a boy," Walt shouts. "Herschel, old friend, you got yourself a beautiful son!"

Walt hands the baby to Chana and Chana lays him on a table of towels and dabs her new nephew, trying to prevent her tears from falling on him. As he squirms and cries she giggles, watching the jerky movements and loving this fresh and perfect child. She studies his features, and is reminded of her grandfather.

Mother Abbot walks to where Chana is wiping the baby. She moves Chana aside and covers the baby in soft linens and carries the bundle into the library, Chana and Father McKay at her heels.

Not sure where he should be standing, Sam Porter joins them. Father McKay lays out holy victuals before he turns to the noisy newborn in the arms of his grandmother.

"Are you Catholic?" Mother Abbot asks Sam Porter.

"My parents were. My mom had me baptized," says Sam.

"What's your name—your full name."

"Samuel H. Porter. Samuel Henry Porter."

"Samuel is good enough."

Chana watches her vocal nephew with wide-eyed interest as Father McKay chants and baptizes the babe.


Walt finishes assisting Amalie, washes his hands, and looks down at her. "You did well, Amalie. Where did you find that last Herculean strength?

"From Herschel's mother," Amalie says, snuggling her pillow.

"My mother?" Herschel asks.

Amalie sleeps.

# CHAPTER 25
## *May 1922*

Layland spots Chana rushing against the crowd to the edge of the platform where they always meet. When he sees her, his heart jumps. Her filmy summer frock with varied-length hem, accentuates her trim figure. He hurries to her, drops his suitcase and scoops her into his arms.

"You smell like heaven," he says. "It makes me weak and strong at the same time. What is it, Jasmine? Rose? Vanilla?"

"It's the Chanel perfume you brought to me last time you were home," she says, putting his arm around her shoulder. "Our taxi is over there."

In the back of the taxi, she tells him about the incredible birth of his nephew between kisses.

"It sounds like everyone was there except me," chirps Layland, kissing her face again.

Chana lays her head on his shoulder. "I have never talked much of my Jewish heritage with you."

"I know, sweetheart. I sort of thought you would tell me when it felt right."

She sits up and cups her hands in her lap. Looking down at them she says, "Amalie thought it would be good to ask Rabbi

Lowenstein to do a ceremony. We need to do our part to show honor to our heritage."

"That should not worry you, sweetheart," he says. "Herschel would do anything to make Amalie feel comfortable."

"I know. In Russia there were pogroms. Our synagogue was burned twice. We could not practice openly. Mother was not Jewish, but she loved the ways of my father's parents. Our grandmother taught us many Jewish traditions, but we are not educated in our religion like other Jewish people."

"You're shy and nervous," he says, stroking her hand. "Everything is all right."

"Rabbi Lowenstein agreed to help us name the baby and perform the Brit – it's a circumcision ceremony. Oh, Layland, I am so sorry I did not tell you about this, but it's the eighth day and it is important that…"

Layland places a finger over her lush, pouty lips as she blinks back the tears.

"Chana, don't you know that whatever is important to you is important to me?"

Chana retrieves a handkerchief from her handbag, wipes her eyes and nose, and lays her head back on Layland's shoulder. "Amalie and I do not feel comfortable going into a synagogue, but the rabbi will do a private ceremony in his home."

"I'm sure that's fine, Chana," Layland reassures, lifting her chin so their faces are close.

Her eyes grow large as her explanation continues. "There's a part for you in the ceremony."

"For me?" Chana nods affirmatively.

"What is it you want me to do?"

"Talk." Chana reaches into her handbag, opens a paper and hands it to him. Layland takes the paper and studies it silently.

He looks back into her uneasy eyes and smiles.

"I'm happy to read this, Chana. Every word of it is true."

Chana smiles and hugs him.

Their taxi bypasses the road homeward and heads for Herschel and Amalie's house.

When Layland enters their home he feels a quiet, sweet difference. His uncle's voice chokes and misty words surface with difficulty.

"Layland, my dearest nephew and brother-in-law. You and I were raised like brothers, and now, thanks to our wives, we are brothers. I can never thank you enough for bringing me Amalie, and now I am a father – can you believe it, I have a beautiful family."

Amalie emerges from the kitchen, cradling the baby in her arms. Herschel draws her close and bends down and kisses his son, then lifts him from her arms.

"My dearest brother, it is my honor to introduce you to your nephew. It is a gift to be an uncle – a gift that your mother gave to me and now I am able to bestow it upon you."

Layland studies the baby, and the boy stretches, opens his frowny eyes and blinks. Herschel passes the infant into Layland's arms, and Layland stiffly balances him. The tiny, warm body smells fresh. Layland studies the miniature features.

Herschel watches the bonding process. "We are naming him today at the rabbi's home. It's a good thing you got here today. There's apparently a timing issue."

"That's what I understand," says Layland. "I have a taxi outside; should we go?"

Amalie slips into her shawl and takes the baby from Layland, re-swaddling him in a white blanket. They close the door behind them and descend the front steps to the waiting cab. Herschel helps Amalie and his infant son into the back seat, walks around to the opposite door and climbs in beside them. Chana and Layland crowd into the front with the driver and Herschel gives the driver directions to the synagogue. When they arrive,

Herschel directs the driver to continue down the driveway to a cottage behind the synagogue. Herschel's friend, Dr. Walter Lawson is waiting in front. Herschel opens the door of the taxi for his wife, takes the baby until Amalie is upright, places him back in her arms and wraps a supportive arm around the small of her back. When they approach their doctor-friend Walt lifts the blanket so he can see the face of the baby and smiles.

"It's okay that you pull baby out, Walt," says Amalie.

Herschel smiles and hugs Amalie closer to him.

"Come in," beckons the rabbi from the front door, ushering the party into his comfortable home. As they are introduced to the rabbi's wife, Layland's eyes are riveted on the surgical instruments laying out on the side table.

"Please come into our parlor and we will talk for a while before the ceremony," invites Rabbi Lowenstein.

When everyone is seated comfortably, the rabbi's wife offers beverages, which everyone declines.

"Layland and Herschel, I would like you to know a little about your wives' heritage," says the rabbi. "Chana's and Amalie's family are Khazarian descendants. Although their mother was gentile by birth, from what I understand, she was adopted into the family of her husband, giving the Meinrel children the privilege of Jewish heritage." Rabbi Lowenstein pauses and sips his coffee. "Your child, Herschel, is Jewish, receiving that birthright through his mother." He takes a breath.

"Let's talk a little about the ceremony. Layland, you will be the Kvatter and Chana you will be the Kvatterin—similar to godparents in the Catholic religion. Walt, you will be the Sandek. The role of Sandek is very sacred. You will hold the baby on your lap during the circumcision, and your lap is compared with the alter of the temple. The honor of Sandek traditionally links your soul with the soul of the baby. I told Herschel and Amalie to choose someone that is a righteous man, who would draw down a holy soul for the child. The child will take his good character traits from you, Walt. You will be his spiritual mentor, so this shows the level of trust Amalie and Herschel have for you."

Herschel leans over and whispers to Walt. "I didn't choose you for exalted reasons of exaltation. I need you to watch his knife." Walt ignores him, so Herschel continues whispering. "Well, I also hope your spiritual values are intact, just in case." Herschel looks at Walt. "Are you crying? Are those tears?"

Walt pokes Herschel with his elbow and wipes his nose. When the rabbi finishes explaining Walt bows his head to the rabbi. "It is an honor, Rabbi Lowenstein. Years ago my wife died and I have no posterity. This child might well be the closest posterity I will ever experience. Thank you, Amalie and Herschel."

The rabbi continues. "We will not be using the minyan today – that is the group of men who form the prayer circle. This will be a small ceremony, and my wife has prepared a meal to follow." The kindly Rabbi studies his new friends, especially Herschel.

"Before we continue, Herschel do you have any questions?"

"Everything about Amalie is important to me. This ceremony makes her feel more connected to her family. My only question is, will this action put limitations on our son's religious choices in the future?"

"Nothing we do today will impact his future decisions. At the end of the ceremony, he will be circumcised, and that is permanent. To us, meaning me, Chana and Amalie, your baby will be given a blessing that will enter him into the covenant of Abraham, the father of us all. You are committing yourselves to teach him, to nurture him, and to be good examples for him—as we previously discussed. This ceremony does not make him more Jewish than he already is."

"Thank you, Rabbi Lowenstein. Our desire is to honor his heritage by teaching him all of it. There's quite a variety."

"Today's ceremony will not limit him. If anything, it will open more doors. It is not easy to be Jewish. As you know, there are prejudices. But your son is already Jewish."

The rabbi looks around. "I'm not sure when I've seen so much consternation on so many faces. A brit is not a dreadful occasion, but a joyous one."

No one moves.

"Amalie, are you ready?" asks the rabbi.

"Yes, Rabbi," Amalie says.

"Chana, do you have the part you and Layland will perform?"

"Yes, Rabbi," whispers Chana.

"Doctor, have you examined the baby and determined him healthy?"

"Yes, Rabbi," says Walt.

"Then, I will prepare for the ceremony. My wife will direct you when it is time to bring the baby into the dining room. Layland, you and Chana will carry him in. Walt, when you come in, I will show you where you will sit. You will need to remove the baby's clothing. There is a covering for him on the table." Walt nods.

The rabbi exits and the group sits quietly for a short time. The rabbi's wife hands traditional kippah's to the men before ushering everyone into the dining area.

The rabbi is wearing a ceremonial robe and kippah and begins chanting in melodious prayerful Hebrew tones. The sounds and tones whisper peace to Amalie's heart as she watches her baby son in the arms of her sister and brother-in-law. The rabbi indicates a chair for Walt to sit, which is next to the empty chair reserved for Elijah. Amalie watches the undressing of her son and Walt's tenderness with him. She watches with interest as the rabbi transfers her baby to the chair of Elijah, chants prayers over him, and transfers him back to the lap of Walt.

The rabbi reaches for tools and Walt opens the covering and exposes the tiny body. The infant jumps slightly, so Walt nestles him. A moment later the baby's scream pierces the air. Herschel and Amalie wince and step closer together. Layland's head lowers and Chana sniffles. The afflicted babe is placed in Amalie's arms and she comforts him.

Now the rabbi speaks in English, to the relief of those present. He pronounces a blessing on the baby and turns to Herschel and Amalie and blesses them with wisdom and the ability to nourish and implant gifts and qualities in the infant.

When the rabbi is quiet, Herschel clears his throat, tries to speak, and clears it again. "We are thankful for this infant who blesses our home and who fills our hearts with joy," he says.

Amalie places the infant in Herschel's arms and lights the Havdalah Candle, speaking words of coming together like the flame, and sparking divinity.

Chana takes the infant and speaks melodiously in practiced English. "We are thankful for our family. We pray this beautiful baby grows in health and joy, and that we will nurture him." She hands the baby to Layland.

Cradling the baby, Layland reads the part Chana prepared for him, translating it into English. "Our hearts swell with love, and we are thankful for the gift of this new life. May our family be stronger and wiser because of this beautiful child. We know he is not our possession, but the borrowing of divinity, and we pray we may encourage, and never dash, his dreams of greatness."

The rabbi speaks. "May Elijah turn the heart of this child to his parents, and the hearts of his parents to this child as they strive together to find truth and happiness." The rabbi lifts the babe. "We are forever mindful of the covenant of Abraham. We are sworn in our commitment with Jacob. Our everlasting covenant lives in the household of Israel." The rabbi turns to Herschel.

Herschel begins his well-rehearsed recitation. He takes his son from Layland and rocks him gently while he speaks. "We joyfully enter our son who shall be known upon this earth as IVAN LAYLAND MEINREL ABBOTT, into the Covenant of Israel through the rite of circumcision."

Layland's head jerks upward when he hears the baby's name. Herschel continues. "Precious child, your mother and I give you this name that you will always be mindful of your heritage. The name 'Ivan' is from your grandfather in Russia. May you be filled with his goodness and courage. The name 'Layland' links you to your uncle, who brought your parents together, playing a pivotal role in shaping this family, and who marked your course forever. The name Meinrel connects you to your past through your mother, and we bless your mind and heart to learn of and find your roots. Your surname, Abbott, bonds you forever to your Father and his ancestry." Herschel lays his whimpering son back into Amalie's anxious arms.

The rabbi nods approval at Herschel. The rabbi lifts the chalice of wine from the table and blesses it, then places a drop of wine on baby Ivan's lips. The rabbi continues the ceremony through the recitation of Birkat Kohanim and the pronouncement of baby Ivan's Hebrew name, and gives the baby another drop of wine. When it ends, the family lingers happily, kissing the head of the suffering babe, who is the center of attention during the meal they share at the generous table of the rabbi's wife. The Lowenstein's congratulate each of them in their performing roles, particularly praising the Catholic men for supporting the heritage of their wives.

Entirely relieved and feeling a little giddy, the group thanks the Lowenstein's and walk to the street to await their taxi.

"My turn to hold my namesake," says Layland, taking the bundle from Amalie. "Ivan Layland Meinrel Abbot. I hope your Aunt Chana and I have a baby as beautiful as you."

Walt places his palm on Layland's shoulder. "Until then, Lay, would it be all right with you if I ask Chana to help me in my medical office? I could certainly use the help."

Herschel takes his son from Layland.

"Her mother was the village doctor in Russia," Layland says. "Chana helped her and I'm sure she would love to be involved with patients, but I don't think she'd want to make coffee and collect payments."

"I already have someone for that, Layland. I'd like her to be my medical assistant, to interact with patients—listen to their needs. It will give her a reason to practice her English and I can think of several people who would benefit from her caring touch."

"Why don't you ask her about it?"

"Thanks. I will."

Rabbi Lowenstein runs up to Herschel. "You must come back inside. I just received a letter from Russia. They found Otto."

# Author's Notes

Nicholas II didn't want to be tsar but he was the only one in his ruling family who understood his leadership weaknesses. In the end he managed to lose his crown, ax the 200-year history of Romanov rule, obliterate the Russian Empire, and see his wife and children murdered by Lenin.

Lenin evolved into Russia's first dictator of the twentieth century, although he couched his dictates under the guise "for the good of the people" or "the masses have decided." To disagree would be selfish and probably treasonous, not to mention suicidal. A fellow Bolshevik, Fanya Kaplan, who once suffered as a Siberian prisoner, shot Lenin three times when he proclaimed himself dictator, but he lived, hopefully with discomfort. Kaplan was shot and then obliterated and then burned. All records of her existence were destroyed, along with anyone who ever knew her. A little information about her has surfaced since 2003. I think I was the first to uncover her existence decades ago in a dusty library. She was a fascinating footnote. After Fanya shot Lenin he became reclusive and wholly paranoid, directing death squads and other major management decisions through close confidants, setting a new management style that Stalin followed.

Because of the Vladimirs' management style along with the perceived power of committee members, there was asset application abuse by those vice-dictators. Skeptics wonder if Russia's amazing secret bunkers, many of which were supposedly never used, were actually the brainchild of an individual committee member.

Stalin's legacy is that of a psychotic murderer. He murdered more people in a shorter time-span than Hitler. His name is associated with the term "mass graves" and he is the author of a reign of terror. He destroyed Jews and Christians as well as their churches, and outlawed God.

Along with terrorizing citizens Stalin enjoyed outstanding bravado. He particularly lauded the accomplishments of pilots and daredevils. Russia had a long-distance flyer (ANT-25) that set a world record. There is gossip as well as frail evidence that there were two long-distance flyers.

*The Untethering*, volume 1:     *Save My Sisters*

*The Untethering*, volume 2:     *Find My Brother*

*The Untethering*, volume 3:     *Look Behind You*

*The Untethering*, volume 4      *Come What May*

# Reading group discussion points and ideas:

1. Does it bother you that the family acts normally amidst daily threats of terror?

2. Why does this starving family help refugees?

3. Is Yosef strong or weak?

4. Why do you think Fedora married Ivan?

5. What do you think of Toppur? Was Fanya a "death woman?"

6. How do oppressed people live free?

7. Should Fanya have told Yosef about Zoë?

8. What do you think of Rabbi Wecht?

9. How did Chingas strike you?

10. Why did the family choose Chingas to protect the children?

11. In chapter 16 there are comments about the Polish Riflemen's Association, which effectively protected the Pols until their guns were taken away prior to WWII. Were they effective? The guns of the Polish people were taken away just prior to WWII. If they had retained them, would history be different?

12. If you were alone, aboard the *SS Sierra Nevada* in 1920, heading for a different country, what decisions would you have made? What do you think of matchmakers?

Made in the USA
San Bernardino, CA
08 January 2020